Belly Button and Other Lush Stories

Anad Trebolt

Acknowledgements

I thank my beloved Creator, God the Father and Jesus my savior for giving me the words to put on paper, the well spring of hope in my heart and the bravado all writers need to pass their baby along the park bench so everyone can see her.

I thank my mother Jeanette, for every book she bought me, every story she read to me and for every second of encouragement and reassurance she still gives. Thank you Ma, a millions times over! And a special thanks to my ever patient husband Rodney, who cleaned under my feet, made sure I ate a meal, and listened to I don't know how many plot theories I dropped on him in the middle of a different conversation. God Bless you baby, for my first lap top, for building my office and for not knocking on the door when it was closed. Thank you for putting up with me! A *love ya madly* to my Aunts, my Uncles, a multitude of cousins, and to my sistaz, Mikki, Marion, Beverly, Marcy, Jacquette, Earline, Karen, Kim, Bridgette, LaTia, Khali, Melvina, Ebony, Tonya, the staff at Kearsley and G-Town home. A big hug and a loving Thank You to my brothers, Darren, Andre, Johnny, Will Jr.(especially you, my beta reading brother!) Eric, Alphonso, and William. To Rae and the Smith family and to Mom and Pop J. To every one of you who listened to my stories, read some of them, or asked me "How's the book going?" You gave me the confidence I needed to keep writing, keep dreaming, and to keep on keepin' on. A big fat MWAAH!

to all of you. A special smile goes out to my big brother Terence. I think of you every day.

I cannot forget Colette down under in Australia! Colette, I want you to know that way back in the beginning, before I knew that all first drafts are complete crap, I had considered hanging it all up. Just write a little and stash it somewhere. Until, one night I was cruising through my emails and found yours, asking about The O Spa. Wow. I couldn't stop smiling. That one email fueled me for another two years. And don't you worry, that particular story is under construction as you read this. Thank you Colette! You are every writer's dream. Also, for my friend Tom, thank you for your kind words over the years.

Thank You, to my editors, Rebecca Grossman, Pam Roller, Wendy Ely, Julie Ganis, and cover designer, Dynasty Bearfield. I'm still woefully ignorant of so much, but you all taught me a lot. Thank you for your professionalism, your guidance, and most of all, for your patience. Without you, this project would surely have been a mess.

And to you dear reader. Thank you for spending a little of your precious time reading these stories. I hope you enjoy them, because this book is for you.

March 2014

List of Pleasures

Zara's Dream

1

Zelda eyed the man on the doorstep.

"Yes, can I help you?"

"My name is Elijah Duncan. Is Zara home?"

Zelda looked him up and down but couldn't remember if he was among the throngs of people who had been coming and going for two weeks. The visitors had finally tapered down to one or two over the last three days and she had been hoping for a day of peace and quiet.

"Are you a friend or one of his family members?" she asked.

"A friend."

"Hold on."

Zelda shut the door, locked it and left him out there. Her sister was in her bedroom, sitting in the large overstuffed chair, staring out at the back yard.

"Zara, there's a guy named Elijah at the door. Do you want me let him in? You feel like talking?"

"Okay."

Zelda waited a moment longer for her sister to turn around, make eye contact, do something. She had been sitting in that chair for hours. Zelda didn't know what to do for her anymore. It hurt too much to watch her. She went back down the hall.

Zelda opened the front door and stood back. "She's in her bedroom." she looked at the shopping bag in his hand. "You can go back there and see her." She reached for the bag. "I'll take that."

"No, thank you. It's for her."

"I'm sure it is, but–" Zelda locked the door and turned around, "just the same…"

Elijah held the bag close to his leg. "I'd like to give it to her myself if I may."

Zelda's eyes narrowed as her nostrils flared, but she led him down the hall to *their* room – it was still *their* room – and stood aside to let him pass. She watched him from the doorway.

Eli put the bag down beside the dresser and laid his jacket on top of it.

He knelt beside her, touched her cheek. "Zara."

She sniffed and turned to him. "Hi."

"I found out when the obit came through, but I wanted to wait until it was appropriate."

"I got your flowers," she whispered. "Thank you."

He picked her up out of the chair and sat back down with her.

Zara pressed her face in his shirt. "I'm lost!" she sobbed. "I'm so lost!"

"No, baby." He put one hand in her hair and pressed her close. "You're not. I'm still here. I'm still with you."

Zelda watched them a moment longer before she pulled the door shut against her sister's grief. She wiped her cheeks on the way to the kitchen. It was two hours before Eli stood in the doorway again.

"If either one of you needs me for anything," Elijah held out his business card. "And I do mean anything. Don't hesitate to call me."

Zelda nodded, took his card and shut the door.

She got in bed with her sister and watched her sleep for a few minutes. Zara had on a new fluffy white bathrobe and a thirsty white towel wrapped around her head. She looked warm and smelled like sweet lemons. Zelda kissed her sister's nose like she used to when they were kids and shared the same room.

"Who is he?"

Zara opened swollen eyes and sighed. "You can't tell a soul," she whispered. "Not yet."

Zelda nodded. It felt like old times. Ever since she had moved away almost thirty years ago, she had missed their secret time together. Zelda settled in next to her baby sister to listen, barely breathing.

"His wife died two years ago." Zara yawned and stretched. "And he was so depressed. At the time I didn't know. I didn't know what was wrong with him. He's not a chatty guy. Not like Freddie. I hadn't heard from Eli in almost three months when I finally got a text. I had been waiting for it but dreading it at the same time. When I got there he was sitting in a chair by the window. Just...just sitting there. He wouldn't answer when I called his name. He was quieter than usual. And he had already drunk half a bottle of Jack. He wouldn't say anything and I was too scared to say anything. He just pulled me into his lap and hugged me. Then he started cryin'. And *that* scared the shit outta me. You see how big he is?"

Zelda nodded again. Saying the man was big was being nice. Elijah wasn't fat but she didn't miss how he had sucked up all the space in the doorway.

"Well, believe me when I tell you that Eli ain't afraid of much," Zara went on. "And there he was, cryin' and holdin' me like he was gonna fall apart if he didn't. I tried to wait him out, 'cause I thought the worst, but he wouldn't answer me when I asked him what was wrong." She sighed, remembering how she had wanted to run out and leave him there, just so she wouldn't hear those words. Not from him.

"So I got myself together and did for him what momma used to do for us when we were little and somebody hurt us so bad that we cried."

Zelda leaned back and frowned. "You gave him a bath?"

"Yup. I got up and looked in the bathroom and lo and behold, there was a spa tub in there. With a shower stall across from it. So I ran hot water in the tub, got it all nice and bubbly for him and dragged his sorry ass in there." Zara paused and pulled the neck of her robe closer as Zelda's eyes narrowed. "I washed him. I washed his hair, shaved his face 'cause he looked like he hadn't done it in two weeks, and then I put him in the shower. The whole time he kept taking a few sips of Jack and he still wasn't talking. But I was starting to feel better about the whole thing by the time I rinsed and dried him off. I lotioned him up and wrapped a towel around his head and helped him get in the bed. I figured it was the last time I was ever gonna see him…" She thought about Freddie and her nose started burning. She sniffed. "I was just glad that I could do that much. 'Cause no matter how selfish I wanted to be, the truth of the matter was that Eli was good to me. And I was glad to be there for him. Whatever it was. So I kissed his cheek and was about to leave when he held onto me and whispered one word."

"What was it?"

Zara smiled. It was a slow, wistful but happy smile. The first one in two weeks. Even though Zelda feared the worst, she didn't care. Elijah was all right with her, forever and ever amen, just 'cause he made Zara smile again.

"Never."

"Never?"

"He knew what I was thinking." Zara's wistful look faded. "I thought it was our last time. And even though I hadn't said a word, he knew I was too scared to ask him if we were over." She closed her eyes and smelled him on her skin, could still hear his voice in her ear. He had always felt like he belonged there. "But he answered me anyway. He said 'never.'"

Zelda was amazed at the look of shame laced with excitement on her sister's face. Zara lowered her eyes before she whispered to her.

"I thought I was a married woman having an affair with a married man, which made him safe, 'cause he had as much to lose as I did. But I didn't know he'd been a widower for the past two years until today. When he came to give me a bath."

"Oh my God," Zelda whispered as she rolled onto her back to stare up at the ceiling. "Oh, my God you were cheating."

"No, Zelda, don't do that!" Zara sat up and wiped her face. "Please don't say it like that! I didn't mean to. Not right away. I was good. I was good for twenty years and then..." She shrugged and got up and walked across the room.

"And then what?" Zelda sat up and looked at her. "You just decided one day, 'I think today's the day I'm gon' give my cookies to another man'? Is that what happened?"

"Zelda, Freddie never knew." Zara lit a cigarette, inhaled the acrid smoke and was grateful for it.

"How do you know he never knew? He's dead now, so it's not like we can ask him!"

"Stop judging me!" Zara yelled across the room. "Just because Myron cheated on you doesn't mean that only devils do it! I know he didn't know 'cause Freddie wasn't the kinda guy who could've kept it to himself!" She sighed and lowered her voice. "I can tell you hundreds of reasons why, but it doesn't change anything. And I don't want it to change the way you feel about me. You're my only sister. And I thought I could share everything with you. But not him. If he hadn't come here, I still wouldn't have told you."

Zelda scooted to the edge of the bed with her face puckered sour. "Why, 'cause you know how I feel about people who cheat?"

"Yes. And because I don't want you to love me any less."

Zelda watched Zara pick up the ash tray and walk over to the arm chair with it.

"I love you just as hard as I did the day momma brought you home." Zelda sighed and stood up. "I'm gonna go make us some tea." She looked at the forlorn woman who used to smile all the time, who used to be filled with so much vitality. "Then you can tell me everything. 'Cause it looks like he loves you. And as much as I hate to say it, I'm glad he came by here today."

2

Zelda put the tray on the bed between them, just like when they were kids, then teenagers and then young women. The ritual reminded her of all the nights they'd spent with each other before first her own, then Zara's wedding. The tray held a teapot, two cups, two saucers and was crowded with shortbread cookies.

"I missed doing this," Zara whispered as she blew into her cup.

"You and Freddie didn't drink tea in bed together?"

"Not with a tray. And only when one or both of us was sick." She loved the way Zelda made tea, full of honey, sugar and lemon. It was thick and hot and extra sweet. "And no matter who made the tea, it never tasted this good."

Zelda glanced over at her sister before she blew into her own cup. "I missed it, too."

"Do you still see him? Myron, I mean. Do you still see him now and then?"

"Not really. Not since Meka went to college. I see him if he goes up there to get her and brings her back. But we've been talking lately. You know…since…" her voice trailed away.

"I know." They sipped in silence before Zara asked: "Are you gonna take him back?" She prepared herself for the tirade of husband-hating insults her sister could spew without a moment's hesitation.

"Well...we'll see." Zelda looked off into a distance only she could glimpse. "It's not so easy. Tryin' to love somebody after they hurt you so bad. But...we'll see."

"I don't want you to be like – I-I don't want you to be alone." Zara wiped her face and tried to shake it. "If you can find a way to make it work..."

"Zara, you're not alone. That man came in here and did what nobody else, not even me or momma, thought of. In just a matter of a minute he got you to confess your heart to him and he answered you *perfect*. He said what every woman wants to hear. And from what you told me he's *been* sayin' it. And I saw the way he was holdin' you. Like you was the most precious thing in the world to him. I don't know how you did it, but you found another person to love you to death. Now you been dancin' around it with this tea, but it's time now. It's just me and you. In our secret time. And I still love you the way I always have. So c'mon and tell me how you managed to become everything in that man's eyes."

Zara sat back against the pillows. Love. What was love but an emotion made to manipulate the senses and cloud one's judgment? Sex had started it, but love finished it. For all of them. Love was the reason her heart ached in every direction. Love was the reason she couldn't decide what to do with herself.

She got started before she lost her nerve.

"I was working on a new project that Amy had been bugging me to finish for a while. It just so happened it was toward the end of my semester and I used the excuse of being a student needing to do some research. I mean, it was true. I was a student, but my classes weren't the reason I was doing the research."

"So you went to him?" Zelda leaned forward to pour herself another cup. "You met Elijah at his job?"

"Yeah. But he wasn't nice at first. And he wasn't very help-ful right away, either. I wound up having lunch with him at least four times, 'cause that was the only time he said he had available. I still didn't get my questions answered. At least not right away."

"Why did it take that long?"

"'Cause he asked more questions than I did. I still remem-ber those weird conversations…"

She had been standing at the security desk almost a half hour before he came out to shake her hand. Elijah was a big bear of a man, fair skinned and frowning, with two hands that envel-oped her one when he pumped it twice.

"Sorry about the wait." Eli said. "I was just finishing up a phone conference and couldn't get away."

"It's okay." He was staring at her like she was a new species and all of a sudden Zara wished she had just left a note and called him from home. "Umm…I just…I just have a few…you know…occupational questions."

"You're working on a project for school, right?" Elijah leaned toward her with a scowl. "That's why you're here, isn't it?"

"Yes!" She hated the panicky sound of her voice. "But if you're busy, maybe I can…" She looked at the door behind her. "I can call you…and…"

Eli narrowed his eyes, took a step closer. "You're here already and I have plenty of time. Let's hear it. What kinda project is it?"

"Its…it's my final grade. We have to come up with a story that's as close to life as possible. It…it should have real street names and…" she shrugged. "I chose to do a piece on a reporter and…she lands a hot story but…sh-she gets into trouble."

He leaned back and relaxed noticeably. After watching her fidget for a few seconds, Eli smiled. "I'm sorry, miss. It's just that people are really nervy these days. It wouldn't be unusual for somebody to come in here and try to see me under false pretenses, since I'm not exactly the first person you'd ask for coming in the door. So–" he shrugged.

"No! I have my syllabus and–"

He smiled at her again. "What's your name?"

"Zara McAllister."

"Zora?" He rubbed his chin. "Like the writer?"

"No. My name is spelled Z-A-R-A. It's pronounced differently. It's not the same."

"Zara. Okay." He nodded. "And as you probably already know, I'm Elijah Duncan, the Editor-in-Chief here at the *Philadelphia Globe*. Pleased to meet you."

Flustered, she shook his hand again.

"In these days and times, a little scrutiny is prudent."

"Okay." She waited for him to ask her over to one of the lobby benches.

Eli started walking toward the door and turned back to her. "I'm on my way to lunch." he said. "We can discuss your project, but I gotta get something to eat."

They walked two blocks to a sushi restaurant where the maître d addressed Eli by name and quickly ushered them to a table for two.

"You're a little old to be a student, aren't you?"

She couldn't believe how rude he was and had to remind herself that he was just an interview. Hopefully a quick one. "One is never too old to be a student."

Eli accepted the menu. "Touché. So how old are you?"

"What? How is my age relevant?"

"If you're gonna write a young cub, you should think like one. And you're too old to think like a twenty-year-old, which means you're not writing one. How old is your reporter?"

"I can write a twenty-year-old if I want to. She's in her thirties. She's not a cub."

Eli watched Zara lay her menu down. He indicated to her when the waiter came to stand beside the table.

"A diet soda, please." she told the waiter.

"The sushi's excellent." Eli said.

"I'm good, thank you."

"You can order tempura if you don't like sushi."

"I'm aware, but no, thank you."

"The food here is very good."

"I've had sushi before, I've been here before, I'm aware that this is a five-star restaurant. It's two o'clock in the afternoon. I've already had lunch and a diet soda will be fine. Thank you." She watched the hint of a smile fold the corners of Eli's mouth as he ordered.

"So I take it you're in your thirties."

"Like I said, what–"

"Then you're in your forties."

"Okay wait a min–"

"I'm just trying to get a feel for this imaginary person that you're writing your story about, but in order for me to really help you, I need to know how good your skills are. Most fiction writers, especially women, tend to write about and for the age group they're in."

She wondered if she'd picked the wrong person. Or even the wrong newspaper. Elijah Duncan was an asshole if God ever created one. "That is seriously sexist and not true."

"I know. I just wanted to see where your head's at." He grinned.

She spent the next forty minutes fending off questions about herself, only to find out as Eli hustled her back up the street toward his office that reporters were trained to use aggressive interviewing skills. And she needed to sharpen hers if she was gonna pretend to be one. On paper anyway.

"I'm available for lunch next Thursday." Eli held out his card. "Be here at one o'clock sharp and bring your appetite 'cause I don't like eating alone. And if I have to wait more than a minute for you, I'm gone."

She stood on the street looking at his card, wondering what just happened.

"I was so…" Zara poured another cup of the steaming sweet tea. "I was so out of practice that I didn't even realize he had started flirting with me until the fourth lunch."

"How in the world did you miss that?"

"I don't know. I guess I wasn't looking for it. I mean…you saw him. He's a tall, handsome, rugged-looking brotha. He's so sure of himself. Every time we went someplace he wanted to eat, women damn near fell on the ground trying to get his attention. What would he want with me?"

"Zara," Zelda snickered. "You're either really clueless or you don't look at yourself much. You're the most beautiful woman I know."

"That's not true and you know it."

Zelda blinked. "Well what happened on the fourth date that made you realize he was attracted to you?" Zelda watched her sister's eyes glaze over as she got lost in the memory of that day. A sweet, endearing smile lit Zara's face. Her eyes sparkled.

3

Zara, frustrated with the "Who's on First?" cadence of their conversations, lost her temper in a parking lot.

"Okay!" She held her hands up. "You haven't answered one question and this is the fourth time we've had lunch together! I'm just about done. Forget it, I don't care if I gotta make this shit up, 'cause I'm not getting anything I need from you–"

"I'm not getting anything I need from you, either," Eli grinned.

"What?"

He grabbed her shoulders and planted a firm kiss on her lips. Zara thought she was having a heart attack as her handbag fell to the ground beside her and the sound of bells rang in her ears. His kiss deepened as he opened her mouth and sent sensations of sweet pleasure rippling up and down her body. His tongue flicked against her upper lip and made her bones rattle before he pulled back and looked at her. Zara stared at him in shock.

"Meet me again and I'll tell you everything you need to hear." he said.

She was so dumbfounded she couldn't answer. She watched him bend down in front of her and scoop up her bag and keys. Her heart was pounding like a pair of congas under the right hands.

"Give me your cell phone number." Eli took her hand, opened it and dropped her keys in it. "Can you receive texts?"

"Yes," she whispered. She recited her number in a daze as he typed it into his phone. "I…" Her hand with her keys in it reached up to her chest, her fingers clutched her shirt.

"I'm gonna send you an address and a time." Eli said. "If you're ready, answer me. If you're not…" He leaned closer and Zara pressed herself against her car as he kissed her cheek. "If you're not then I'll understand."

She nodded as he took her keys from her and opened her car door. She got in and turned the engine over. When he leaned toward the window she rolled it down.

"Zara."

She could hardly take in a breath. "Yes?"

"I love to hear you say that word."

She screeched out of the parking lot with her mouth open in an O.

Three days later her phone vibrated as she sat on the back porch in front of her laptop. She picked it up and prayed it wasn't Amy. Her agent was beyond persistent. But it wasn't a call, it was a text. *21 North Juniper Street at 9pm.* She frowned and looked up the address online.

"Oh shit." Zara pushed her chair back, looked from her phone to her laptop and back to the phone again. She had typed in the right address. "Oh shit," She picked up her phone and went to pour herself some wine. "Oh shit, oh shit." She gulped down half a glass and thought about him as she looked at the address.

Eli was handsome, that much was true. He wore a wedding ring but didn't talk about his wife or his kids, which was okay as far as she was concerned because she didn't care to know. He was intelligent. He liked to eat his lunch at a table with a cloth napkin instead of a paper one. But sex? With him? Naked with a man she didn't really know?

16

"Oh shit." Zara poured herself another half a glass and downed it. She licked her lips and remembered the way it felt when Eli had done the same. "Oh my God."

It was also true that she was so sex starved that just two weeks ago she had flown to Colorado to meet Freddie at his hotel room just to get some. Only to come back completely disappointed because her husband was so tired from working day and night on his contract that all he could manage was three pumps before he passed out.

And then Elijah kissed her. It was a real kiss. Not a quick, 'Okay honey I'll see ya in a few weeks I gotta go' kiss. But a real live, 'I'm gonna fuck your brains out if I get the chance' kiss. And it was also true that she needed her brains fucked out in a serious kinda way. "What in the hell..." She poured a full glass of wine and drank half of it. "Am I gonna do about this?"

Before she could answer herself her fingers made the decision.

Yes.

Zara drank half the bottle and got dressed in a wine-induced haze. She didn't remember putting on the lacy panties with the butterfly on the front or the button-up blouse with the deep v that exposed her cleavage above her favorite black skirt. She barely remembered going into her office to pick up the red gauze pouch that held all the condoms she got at the city clinic from her last research project.

She remembered listening to Marvin on her mP3 during the cab ride. But walking through the lobby of the vast hotel was blur.

"Ms. McAllister, Mr. Duncan has requested that we make him aware of your arrival. Is now a good time?" the thin-lipped young man behind the desk asked her. She told him that it was and he handed her the room key. Thin lips droned on and on about the room's amenities before he directed her to the upper floor elevators and bid her an enjoyable stay.

The shower was running when she got there. Zara stood just inside the door and told herself to buck up. She barely noticed the elegant cherry wood furniture or the plush carpet that cushioned the sounds of her foot steps in the anteroom. She glanced at the large bed on the other side of another open door before she turned around and spotted the full ice bucket with a bottle of champagne in it next to a bottle of Jack Daniels.

She frowned at the champagne and poured herself a shot before she put her headphones back on in time to hear the end of Floetry's live version of *Say Yes*. She contemplated what she was doing as she looked out onto the courtyard below.

Eli took just long enough for her to consider leaving. Maxwell's *'Till the Cops Come Knockin'* had ended and *Wey U* began when she turned around and reached for her clutch.

Eli walked toward her wearing a towel around his waist. She was instantly glued to the spot. The Latin drums got their thing going in her chest as his hands reached out to her. She lowered her eyes when he removed her headphones.

"Every time I see you, you take my breath away." he said.

The drums revved up a few notches when he kissed her cheek. She couldn't look at him and was so grateful when he took her hand and looked at her mP3.

"Hot tub mix?"

She nodded. "Some of my favorite songs are on there." She couldn't believe she was talking normally. He paused the player and reached his hands around her back to the small table behind her.

"What are you drinking?" he murmured in her ear.

"J-jack."

"Good choice."

She stepped aside while he poured himself a shot, his eyes watched hers above the rim of his glass as he sipped.

"I'm glad you're here." he said.

The small bit of nerve she borrowed from her drink left her, she nodded silently as her gaze fell. She looked up again to find his eyes regarding her cleavage. He picked up the bottle before he walked away.

"Come," he tossed over his shoulder.

She emptied her glass in one gulp and followed him into the bedroom.

Eli sat on the bed and reached for the mP3 player still in her hand, he placed it in small speaker dock. Zara couldn't move another inch. Just hopping into bed with him was impossible!

She did a quick half-turn, intending to burn a path in the carpet on her way to the door. Eli grabbed her hand and pulled her back.

"Are you nervous?"

She nodded, hoping her eyes didn't fall out of her head.

"So am I."

"You are?" she whispered.

"Yeah." Eli started unbuttoning her blouse and looked over at the radio as Zoe Spencer's *Come To Me* serenaded them. "That's nice."

Zara's blouse sailed down to the carpet behind her as the drums beat a furious staccato in her chest. She covered herself with her hands.

"Why would you think I'm not?" He reached behind her for her skirt's zipper. "You think I've done this before, don't you?"

She nodded silently as her zipper did a slow dance down to its source.

"Nope." Eli shook his head. "I never even considered something like this until I met you."

"But–" Her skirt fell to the floor and Zara held her breath as she watched him look at her body.

"Damn," he whispered. "I thought you were beautiful with clothes *on.*"

She shivered as his hands ran up and down her hips during the sexiest kiss she had ever endured. Eli's tongue teased and explored her with astounding audacity. Zara wrapped her arms around his shoulders and melted into him. She didn't feel his fingers on her back until her bra fell away. She gasped and put a hand to her chest.

"Uh-uh," he told her as his hands caressed her shoulders. "I don't wanna miss anything about you."

Her bra hit the floor, the condom snapped in place, and within seconds Zara was on her back, moaning in sweet ecstasy. Marvin Gaye's *Come Live With Me* encouraged them in the background as his fingers moved slowly inside her while his mouth plundered hers. His thumb strummed her into a state of mindless pleasure and Zara arched her body and begged for more until Eli pushed her thighs apart and penetrated her in one smooth, upward stroke.

Zara gasped and held it in as her body slowly accommodated him. It wasn't that she felt him all the way to her lungs, no that wasn't it at all. It wasn't that he was wide, broad or even big. The issue was that he was simply voluminous. She could hear herself breathing in short little bursts because he took up the space she needed to inhale properly.

"I'm not gonna hurt you," he whispered. "I promise I won't hurt you."

Eli turned onto his side and brought her with him. Zara whimpered as she felt him shift and spread her further still.

"Won't hurt you..." They faced each other and he kissed her as his fingers touched her between them and he stroked her slowly. "I promise..."

Zara gasped over and over again as Eli moved his hips against hers. His fingers manipulated her until she moaned and her body trembled. Every stoke was heaven, his kiss was bliss delivered. As the sexy sounds of Marvin Gaye coupled with the resonance of their undeniable pleasure, Zara climaxed all over him. Eli kissed her nose and reached beside him to hit the repeat button before he turned and flipped her onto her back.

"Oooh!" She clutched his shoulders as he covered her mouth with his own.

She struggled for breath as he swelled inside her and moved with an ever-increasing fervor. She closed her eyes, held on as he pulled her closer with one hand at the middle of her back and stroked her relentlessly. He was so good she could barely stand it. While Janet's *Rope Burn* played softly, Eli slowed down and gave her the most intense and sensual grind of her life.

He fed her fruit. They drank more Jack. He did things to her that was so incredible that even the next day as she sat soaking in her tub, Zara put her hand over her mouth in disbelief.

"When did you see him next after that?" Zelda asked her as she picked up a cookie. "Was it right away?"

"No." Zara put her cup down and lit a cigarette. "I couldn't. I couldn't believe that I had even done it once. Even though he would only text me once a week, he was persistent and I couldn't work. It got so I could barely think straight."

"Was he harassing you?"

"No. It was just one word."

Zelda envied the dreamy look on her sister's face.

"*When.*" Zara took a drag and blew circles in the air above them. "That's all he wanted to know. When."

4

Zara looked at her phone before deleting the question, the same way she did the Friday before. And the Friday before that and the Friday before that one. She desperately wished Freddie would come home to distract her from what she was thinking, but his part of the job wouldn't be over for at least another thirty days. She opened the calendar on her phone and looked at the dates. She flipped back to her instant messages and typed "Tomorrow". Too nervous to wait for a response, she put the phone down and went to make herself a cup of tea and grab a smoke. What was she thinking, saying "Tomorrow"? Agreeing to another night of wild sex?

"Yup," she answered herself as she pulled a mug down from the shelf. "That's what I'm doing. Agreeing to another night of wild sex." She sighed when the phone chimed in the other room. "But this is the last time. After this, I'm just gonna have to buy a vibrator or something." She poured the boiling water into the cup. "Something that kisses me the way I wanna be kissed, licks my fingers and sucks my toes and makes me come all night with the best sex I've ever had in my life!" Zara giggled. "Oh, God! I gotta find a vibrator that does all that!"

Her phone revealed an address and time. She frowned and took a drag before she sat down to look up the address on the web. Another hotel. She picked up her phone. *Yes.*

Zara's nerves were a jangled mess even though she had two shots of tequila before she left the house. The booze helped her glide through the dimly lit, discreetly expensive art deco lobby. Elijah was pouring himself a drink when she walked in. Again, he wore nothing but a towel. She let the door close softly behind her as she looked at his expansive back and wondered if she had left finger nail marks in it the last time.

"I'm having Dewars tonight," he said as he half-turned toward her. "Would you like one?"

She laid her bag down on a chair midway in the room. "Okay." She took a healthy sip as he watched her. "Are you upset that I took so long to answer you?"

"No." He shook his head. "Curious though."

Zara lowered her eyes and tried to make her lips tell him that they wouldn't be doing this shit again after the night was over.

"I couldn't stop thinking about that night," Eli took a step closer. "And how incredible you felt."

"I…" She closed her eyes and sighed when he leaned down to nuzzle her ear. "I can't…"

"I need to know," he whispered as he walked her to the bed behind them. "I need to know how you taste."

She gasped when she felt his hands under her skirt, then under her panties. With a cunning speed that she couldn't believe, he had unzipped her skirt and picked her up off her feet. He kissed her as he laid her on the bed and when he pulled her panties down, his face followed them.

"No!" She sat up and tried to stop him. Doing something like that was so, so personal. It was coveted and shared only between lovers. Not two people on a booty call. "Don't!"

"I want you to come for me." Eli leaned down and kissed her face until she relaxed. Once she did, first his hands then his shoulders pushed her thighs apart. "Oh, my God, you smell good." He licked the inside of her thighs as she trembled. "I want you to come for me all night."

Zara tried to control herself as Eli licked her slowly and she moaned helplessly under such exquisite expertise. She clutched the sheets in her fingers as he draped her thighs over his shoulders and his tongue explored the sticky, sweet inside of her body. Leisurely, Eli licked her from the bottom to the top, where his lips fastened on her sweet spot. He suckled and pulled and teased her until her body arched and her buttocks filled his palms. Zara covered her mouth with the back of one hand as sounds she'd never made before escaped her without license. She found herself panting and whimpering as his fingers invaded her, coming and going rapidly as his tongue matched their rhythm.

Never in her life had she felt such pure and unadulterated pleasure. Sparks flew wildly behind her eyes as she became so wet and so stimulated that she cried out and exploded in his face. She could barely catch her breath as he moved on top of her and she tasted herself in his kiss for the first time.

"Once a month," Eli whispered as he unbuttoned her blouse. "I have to have you at least once a month. Don't deny me. I need you."

Zara wrapped her arms around Eli's neck as he filled her with the sweetest pleasure of her life. "Yes!" She cried out as they moved with each other in an earth-shattering rhythm. "Yes!"

"We got together once a month for amazing sex and then went back to our lives afterwards. We both admitted on more than one occasion that we couldn't wait for the next time.

"I kinda tucked him away in the back of my mind and would only think about him when I was alone. 'Cause we weren't…

you know, like confidants for each other or anything. So we… we went on like that for almost a whole year until…"

Zelda got up and moved the tray to the dresser. "Until what?"

Zara chewed the edge of her lip. "He brought handcuffs with him one night."

"And?" Zelda watched her sister light another cigarette with shaking hands. "What happened with the handcuffs, Zara?"

5

They appeared out of nowhere like a nasty magic trick. Eli clapped one end neatly over her wrist.

"What are you doing?" Zara screeched. She tried to pull her wrist out of his grasp, but it was too late. "Take it off!"

"Wait a minute," Eli grinned. "We're gonna do something a little different."

"No!" She tried to fight the band of panic squeezing her chest. Horrified, she watched him bring his arm closer to hers as he opened the other end of the cuff. "Don't do that!" She pulled her arm with all the strength she had. "Take it off!

"Hey!" He leaned back and looked at her. "Okay."

"Now!" She tried to jump off his lap. "Takeitoffgetitoffgetitoff! Nownownowno–"

"Zara!"

She hung her head and fought for each breath as she squeezed her eyes shut over the tears. "Please! Please, just–"

"Okay!" Eli grabbed the key off the nightstand.

Zara jumped off his lap and tried to take her arm with her. "It's okay, honey. I'm gonna take it off right now."

"Please!" She couldn't help the whimpering. Somewhere in the back of her mind was the thought to open the door behind him, but he still had her arm in his grip.

The cuff popped open and Eli grabbed her when she tried to run past him. "I'm sorry!" He hugged her as she covered her face. "I'm sorry baby, I'm sorry."

She pushed him back and ran for the window.

"ZARA!" He yanked her away from it just as she tilted her head as far back as she could and started wheezing. "Okay. I'll open the window but you gotta stay away from it." Eli grabbed her chin and pulled her face back to him. "Can you hear me?"

She nodded before he let her go and he hurried over to the window and threw the sash up. He held her hand as she stood a foot away from it and let the cold air blow in her face.

"We're gonna step back," he said.

Zara shook her head as she pulled in great whopping gulps of air.

"Just long enough for me to get a blanket." he said.

Together they backed away from the window until Eli could reach behind him and pull one off the bed. He wrapped the comforter around the two of them as Zara faced the night air in his arms. After a while her breath came slow and even.

"Better?" he asked.

She nodded.

"Panic attack?"

Zara shrugged and closed her eyes against the wonderful chill that caressed her cheeks, her mouth, her nose.

"Before just now, who else handcuffed you?"

When she didn't answer, Eli turned her to him. "Zara." His face was stern. "Who handcuffed you?"

She shook her head and looked past him at her clothes on the hanger beside the bed.

"Was it your husband?"

"No!" She tried to get out of the blanket but Eli held her with a hand against her back. "Nobody handcuffed me. It's ancient history. It was over twenty years ago."

"There's nothing ancient about what just happened here." he looked at her closely. "Who was it?"

She sighed. "I don't wanna talk about it. Can we just let it go?"

"No." He walked the two of them to the chair beside the window. "You scared the hell outta me and I gotta know what boundaries you have." He sat down and pulled her onto his lap. "Tell me what happened over twenty years ago. I need to know."

Zara laid her head on his chest and after a few moments of silence, she told Eli about a boy she thought she liked when she was away at college. This boy (for he was barely eighteen himself) took her to the movies, met her after classes, bought her lunch and dinner and claimed to like her, too. One night, Zara's roommate told her she was going to the library. The boy mistook the alone time as an opportunity to have sex. When Zara refused, the boy got mad. He slapped her. She got mad and punched him in his eye, then the boy grabbed her wrists with one hand and tried to strangle her to death with the other.

"I couldn't even scream," Zara whispered. "I was so lucky that the library was closed and my roommate came back. He didn't even notice that she was trying to get him off me." She turned her face into his chest. "She had to...she had to knock him out her text book."

"Jesus Christ!" He hugged her tighter. "What happened after that? Did you report it?"

"No. We were so scared that he was dead, we dragged him out and left him on another floor. I couldn't leave my room for days. A week after that I was home. For good."

"Oh, Zara, you should've reported him." Eli wiped her cheeks with his hand. "That's assault, attempted rape and attempted murder. He needs to be behind bars."

"I was only nineteen. What did I know about the right thing to do?"

"Baby, I'm sorry. I'm so sorry."

Zara leaned back and looked up at Eli. "I like it when we hold hands. But—you can't hold my wrists, you can't tie me up, you can't bind me in any way, in any direction. It scares me."

Elijah promised he never would again. They sat together in the chair for a long while.

"I think we became friends that night," Zara admitted as Zelda watched her with her mouth hung open. "I wanted to leave after that, but he begged me to let him make it up to me. It was the sweetest, most gentle time we ever had."

"Zara!" Zelda jumped off the bed and walked across the room, wringing her hands. "I can't believe you never told me about that!" She turned around with tears in her eyes. "I can't believe you never told *anybody!*"

"I couldn't." Zara put a hand on her forehead. "I just wanted it to go away. And it did. I graduated right here and nothing like that ever happened again. I was fine. I'm still fine. I just...I just can't do the handcuff thing."

"Oh, my God!" Zelda threw herself on the bed. "Aww Jesus!"

"Zelda, you gotta swear you'll keep that shit to yourself."

When her sister didn't answer right away, Zara leaned over and shook her. "Swear it, Zee!"

"All right, I swear it."

"It was twenty-five years ago. You better keep your lips zipped."

"I will." Zelda gave her sister a forlorn look. "I need some more tea."

"Yeah, me too."

A half hour later, each sister sipped in silence for a few moments.

"So you just kept seeing him once a month until the day his wife died?"

Zara snorted. "Not exactly. I didn't know his wife died. All I knew was that six weeks had passed and I hadn't heard from him. And then another three weeks came and went. I called his job and asked if he was there, but when his secretary put me on hold while she went to get him, I hung up."

"Why didn't you talk to him?"

"Because Zee, he hadn't called me for a reason. Something was wrong and I just wanted to be sure that he was still alive and kickin'. For all I knew his wife had found out or some shit. I wasn't trying to make matters worse by acting like a hysterical mistress. Besides," she took another sip, "our agreement was once a month. Just sex and conversation. We didn't go out to lunch or dinner, we didn't go to the movies or shows and we didn't celebrate holidays together. We were not a couple. So, when he didn't call me for almost three months, I thought it was over."

"Just like that? Thirty-six months of sex and see ya?"

Zara nodded and remembered how she felt like her head was going to pop off when she realized that Eli was okay. "Yeah. Just like that."

"But after you gave him his bath and everything, after he realized that you thought it was over, he told you never."

"Yeah." She had made a vow to herself the day she held and comforted Eli in the bathroom, wiped the tears off his face and finally got him settled, that once she got in the car she could howl her head off. But he made it all okay when he said the word she so desperately needed to hear.

"And the two of you went back to your schedule?"

"Well, it wasn't that easy for him." Zara shrugged. "After that, I told him I needed a minute."

"Damn." Zelda looked at her with admiration. "What'd he say?"

"You need a minute?" Eli said. "For what? A minute away from me?"

"Yes. I need a minute away from you."

"Because I took one?"

Zara turned aside. "It was a little longer than a minute, Eli."

"Don't do this." He put his hands on her shoulders. "Do not tell me that you need a minute. What exactly are you saying?"

"Okay, can we agree to space this out to every two months?"

"Hell no, I'm not agreeing to that shit!"

"Why not?" she shouted.

"Because I love you!" he yelled. "I have since the first moment I saw you. I've been hooked on you since you shook my hand. Why do you think I was blabbering like a fuckin' idiot during all those damn dates we had?"

Zara frowned. "We never went on a date."

Eli rolled his eyes. "We had lunch! We had lunch dates once a week for a month! Don't tell me you don't remember!"

"Of course I remember! But you were…"

"I couldn't just answer your questions and let you walk outta my life." He put his arms around her. "And I still can't. No matter what happens, I'll never be ready for that."

Zara lowered her head but Eli tilted her chin, wiped her cheeks.

"I thought—I thought I was dying!"

"I'm sorry, baby." He kissed her. "I went through a little something, but every day gets better. I don't ever want you to think that I don't love you."

"So we saw each other still." Zara said. "But it was different. There were times when I cried when I came home. And sometimes it took a few days before I answered him. But I always did."

Zelda nodded and thought of her sister differently. Her life wasn't as easy as it looked.

"Today he told me he had been alone all that time and just looked forward to me once a month. He told me he would wait, the way I had waited for him. He said he'd wait all his life if he had to."

"Wow." Zelda finished her tea and thought about that. "So what did you say? Did you answer him?"

Zara could still feel Eli's touch on her skin. "He undressed himself. Undressed me. His hands were so soothing and so gentle. There I was, cryin' like it was *my* life that was over. That was all I could do. That's when he told me she had been gone so long he could scarcely remember feeling the way I do now. He said…" she sighed. "He said at the time he wanted to walk away from me 'cause he thought he owed her memory that much. But then he found out at the morgue that she didn't die alone. There was a passenger in her car with her when she crashed. The man's wife was there to claim his body. Said she knew about them, but her husband wouldn't let the affair go.

"Eli said he couldn't believe it. He didn't know what to do with himself. For two and a half months he owned it. He felt responsible for the way he and his wife had kinda wandered away from each other without trying. He told me the guilt damn near killed him until all he could think about was how he was so alone with it. That was when he knew he couldn't carry it another day. And he called for me." She blew her nose.

32

"But you know what? He's right. That's where I am right now. I feel like, you know, maybe if I had paid more attention to Freddie, if—if I had begged him to stay home" Her voice broke and she covered her face.

"Zara!" Zelda grabbed her sister's hands. "You ain't got nothin' to do with that! That stroke was comin' whether it was here at your side or out in the world somewhere. It was comin' no matter what. And Freddie didn't just work to provide for you. He *loved* his job. He loved it so much that it was nothing for him to pack a bag and leave you here to live without him." Zelda shook her head. "That wasn't you at all, baby. You had nothing to do with it.

"So now that Eli has laid himself bare at your feet, do you love him? That's the question, 'cause he done already told you he'll wait all his life for you. I'm so sorry to tell you this, but what you and Freddie had – that's over now. All that's left are your tomorrows. They can be whatever you want them to be. But you gotta know yourself before you take another step. So…" Zelda cupped her sister's face in her hands. "Do you love him?"

"Yes!" Zara sobbed and leaned her head on Zelda's shoulder. "With everything in me, yes! Am I wrong? Am I wrong?"

Zelda hugged her, patted her back.

"You're the only one who knows. Don't worry. You take your time and you'll get yourself together one day and come up with an answer."

Zelda went home a few days later. She visited once a week with groceries, made sure that Zara ate and helped her make out checks for the bills. When she left each Wednesday, Zara's home cocooned her once more in a warm blanket of tea and wine-buffered sadness as she listened to sorrowful songs and flipped through old photo albums.

Healing came slow. Forgiveness even slower. Her junk mail piled up and the phone rang constantly as life went on beneath the winter's distant sun. Most days she cried on the couch, in the shower, on the back porch, at her desk and sometimes just standing still in the middle of a room, unsure of what she was supposed to be doing. At night she dreamt.

Every night, she dreamt.

A warm breeze caressed her cheeks and lifted her hair off her neck as she stood outside six months later.

Zara looked down at her shoes and couldn't believe the places her feet had taken her over the years.

She raised her hand but quickly pulled it back against her chest and turned around to look up at the blue, blue sky.

The hinges creaked behind her and she turned back to see Elijah standing on his doorstep. Neither of them spoke for a minute.

"I had a dream about you." she confessed. "We were happy."

For Ebony Smith

Tie Me To The Moon

Prologue

When I was a teenager I went to the movies a lot. Sometimes with my family, sometimes with my girlfriends, and as I got older and my body began to develop into what it looks like today, I went with a date. I always went for the horror films.

Then, I couldn't have told you why I loved those ridiculously low-budget flicks, but the attraction was there nonetheless. I loved the squirmy, anxious feeling I got when the monster stood behind the heroine, about to rip her clothes off and do something completely verboten to young and innocent Suzie Chapstick.

I loved leaning into the safe haven of whoever I was with as my nerves stood at attention and the whole world was hushed into a vacuum below the drumming sound of my racing heart. Because in those moments, I was actually breathlessly aroused with apprehension and completely alive.

Looking back, I guess I never really stopped chasing the high I got from gooseflesh and the hair on my arms standing on end in the dark.

C enter City is chock full of bars and night clubs adorned with bright lights, booming music, and young people streaming past brass poles strung with the protective velvet ropes like the ones you used to see in banks. They run around in tight pants, miniskirts and three-inch heels, crowned in a hard layer of mousse, gel and make-up as they laugh loudly or stagger through a black door looking for a place to chuck the greasy burger that's offending all the beer swimming in their guts.

But if you're like me, mid-thirties, nowhere close to gregarious, and prefer *not* to be constantly hit on by a guy named Malik or Chaz (proud of his recently legal right to PAARTAAY and nail the nearest cougar), there are plenty out-of-the-way watering holes for working stiffs and respectable drunks. *If* you know where to look.

Since I live on the 1400 block of Locust, the watering hole I frequent – aptly named The Watering Hole – is on the 1300 block of Sansom Street. It's a two-story establishment with a bar on both levels, but the one on the first floor has a kitchen in the back, so you can order chicken fingers, wings and fries. You know, the sort of food you can pick at if you have a companion with you to share your pitcher of margarita or frozen daiquiri.

During the week the atmosphere is cool and mostly quiet, just the way I like it. And once in a while, on Tuesdays, I take my wine upstairs to the living room-like atmosphere and sink into an overstuffed couch or armchair to listen to erotic poetry or equally raunchy short stories.

I don't do it often, only two or three times in the last year actually, because before I met Mr. Excitement, there was no one for me to push my wet crotch onto after listening to all that talk about stiff dicks and juicy pussies. But you get my point, right? Out-of-the-way, dim, discreet.

I met Edric at The Watering Hole on a calm Tuesday night in June, when there were only four or five other patrons scattered up and down the length of the polished wooden bar. Although he had a great job as an up and coming ad exec, he worked part time at The Watering Hole and, I learned months later, took the job to get over his last girlfriend. She had left him with a broken heart and after months of solitude he decided to get out and away from himself.

I took my favorite seat on the corner stool not too far from the door in case I was feeling courageous and had a little more than my usual. Before I could get my bearings and figure out if it was a Jack Daniels night or if I wanted to hear myself think, there was a giant standing in front of me.

"Do you know what you like?" he asked with a sly grin.

He has dark, enigmatic eyes and a broad face that's pleasing to gaze at. His expression said he wanted to rip my blouse off and I probably would've been offended if it weren't for the slow smile spreading across his sensual lips.

Oh my.

I ordered what had been on my mind since the dreary, post-lunch weekly meeting. "Moscado."

He nodded and reached down to pull up a chilled bottle as our eyes locked. I was spellbound and couldn't look away as he poured my wine and placed the flute on a black napkin.

"That's on me." he said "Don't go away."

I watched him walk to the other end of the bar and serve a few other people as I sipped the cool sanity in my glass. It was wet, semi-sweet, a gentle reminder that I was still on planet earth. Wine was normal. But the sudden turn-on by this complete stranger was not. Every man I'd ever dated or fantasized about was not much taller than me, and certainly not much bigger. And I'm just a few inches above than the fashion standards of petite if you wanna know the truth.

So I was surprised when I got moist watching his expansive back flex below broad shoulders as his wide hands went about the business of pouring forgetfulness into a snifter. I sipped slowly and licked my lips when I noticed his strong, thick legs pushing against the fabric of his jeans when he squatted to get a crystal glass. Even the sight of his unpolished leather boots hardened my nipples as his heavy footfalls pressured the wood floor.

I tossed back the rest of my wine. The sound of my vibrator tugged at the back of my mind. I slung my handbag over one shoulder.

"Not yet."

I looked up and froze. He was pouring me another.

"I have to go," I murmured.

"Not just yet." He shook his head, his eyes penetrating mine. "It's still on me."

He walked away. I sipped and thought, *Okay, another free glass.* I continued to watch him serve other customers, watched him glance at me every now and then and nod. I was just about done when he came back and pulled the bottle up again. I covered the top of the glass with my palm.

"No, thank you." I tried to soften the blow with a gentle smile.

He just stared at me, then silently moved my hand away and gave me an almost imperceptible shake of his head. As if to say, "No, you can't refuse," which was just crazy all by itself. I watched in mute fascination as he filled my glass for the third time. We stared at each other with the wine between us like an unspoken dare, until I couldn't take it. I looked away, not really sure what was happening.

I was turned on, but it felt weird. I should've just jumped off the bar stool and high tailed it outta there. I mean seriously, what was he gonna do? Run after me and insist that I drink it on the street?

My heart was pounding as I practically *gushed* in my panties and felt like I had just finished a power walk. I was flushed and a little breathless. I looked up to find him still staring at me, grinning a little. He put the bottle away as I eyed his chest and imagined it bare and pressed against me. I was so wet I almost squirmed in my seat, but I closed my eyes for a second before I reached for the glass. He smiled before he left me again.

I finally slipped away when he went to the back to get a bottle of something another customer had asked for. When I let myself into my apartment, I couldn't get my jeans undone quick enough, and almost exploded under my own fingers as I peeled off my saturated panties.

I thought about him incessantly. When I woke up in the morning, as I stood naked before the mirror and looked for flaws, in the shower with a soapy washcloth, and afterwards when I massaged lotion over my skin. I imagined the way he felt every night as I lay in bed in the dark. More than the imagined way he felt, I loved the way he made me feel.

Anxious. And just a little shaky. Like when I was younger and went to the movies. For some reason he brought to mind those almost forgotten, lusciously forbidden emotions. For the rest of the week I constantly bit my thumbnail with indecision, but touched myself to fruition on three occasions as brazen images of the two of us together flashed behind my eyes. At night I'd lie in bed, naked and needy, enticed by the memory of his image, helplessly drawn to the thought of him, just as water is pulled by the magnetism of the moon.

I went back.

It was fairly early on Saturday night and there were two bartenders on duty. He was standing opposite my favorite stool when I walked in.

"I'm glad you're back." Edric smiled when I took my seat and he commenced pouring my wine. "I was waiting for you."

Oh my God, you have no idea. I looked at my lap and struggled for composure before I gazed into those mysterious eyes.

"Why?"

"Because I'm just the man you should be dating."

"And you think this because?" I fought a healthy shiver and couldn't tell if I pulled it off or not as the cool silk in my glass slid down the back of my throat. *Easy, Nina. Take it real easy.*

"Because it's true."

I didn't answer him, just slid a twenty across the bar. He stared at me and slid it back. We had another one of those timeless moments when I should've said something smart, but my sharp wit was back at my apartment watching a sitcom with a bag of microwaveable popcorn for company. I took a sip and put the glass down.

"My name is Nina." I introduced myself in one rushed breath.

"Edric."

He held his hand out for a shake and I actually *hesitated!* God help me, my first thought was that touching him would be like holding hands with a lightning bolt. He waited a few seconds until I put my trembling fingers in his. His hand was warm, his palm was soft. I relaxed just a little.

Someone signaled for him toward the middle of the bar. I had only been in there a few minutes, but my panties were already sticking to me and my nerves were humming like live wires.

We were playing a game I was unfamiliar with. I was out of my depth and knew it. I took another sip and quickly slipped out. I made it maybe five steps beyond the wheelchair ramp when I turned around to the hand on my arm.

"You're leaving." He frowned.

I couldn't get my thoughts together enough to find a way to say it. How he excited and scared me at the same time, how I so desperately wanted to rub bellies with him, but...

"I..." I shook my head and started to walk away again.

He pulled me back and put those huge hands in my hair and leaned down to me. Our noses were just a hair's breadth away from each other and I felt close to a swoon for the first time in my life.

"Tomorrow. We'll go out to dinner tomorrow."

"But–"

"Don't say no." He leaned in a little more and our lips almost met. It was the sexiest move any man had ever put on me. I was completely breathless as I waited for a kiss. "Be here at seven p.m."

I was barely able to whisper "Okay."

Edric was completely different at dinner the next night. He was congenial, smiled often, and was a total gentleman. He told me he loved my name, Nina Transome. He said it fit me and reminded him of "a lot of things" – he didn't elaborate further. I left that alone since I wasn't sure I wanted to know. After coffee, since we were only on Broad Street, he walked me home.

I stood outside my building and fished for my keys, stalling for the kiss I needed. The kiss would tell me if he was worth a second date or not. If it was horrible, I would definitely have to start buying my own Moscado, at least until I found another discrete place to have a glass. I found my keys and looked up at the patiently teasing expression on his face.

Fuck it. "Why do you think we're compatible?" I asked.

That ominous, heavy look was back in his eyes and I have to say, after not having seen it all night, I had started to wonder if he was bipolar.

"Because we're opposites."

What? What the hell is that? "I don't get you."

"We each have what the other needs."

I shook my head and made a decision right then and there that I didn't need the kiss. He, and he alone, wielded a mighty pull on my nether regions that I *could not* deny, but I had to be honest with myself, dude was weirded out, which is probably what made him a little exciting. But he was still weird. And nobody needs that.

"There's something about you." Edric moved closer and I looked away as my keys pressed into my fingers. "That lets me know anything is possible."

I lost my breath and looked at my shoes as I shook my head again. *No.*

I'm not an openly defiant person. I'm probably what most people would consider passive, or when I'm angry, passive aggressive. But, the way he spoke to me that night made me shiver somewhere deep inside myself. I suddenly didn't want any more cryptic comments, not one more elusive sentiment.

I wanted the nice, predictable, kinda-needy guys I was used to. I wanted the norm again. Not this brooding Goliath who excited me even as he stirred something hidden in the depths of my soul. *No.*

Edric put a finger under my chin and lifted my face to his. I closed my eyes as my heart thundered and blood pounded in my ears.

"Look at me," he said.

I opened my eyes and my chest hitched. His eyes were smoldering with a fiery intensity that rooted me to the spot.

"When the time comes." He leaned in and his mouth hovered close. "You'll understand me. And I know you're gonna enjoy it."

He pressed his lips over mine and I closed my eyes. He was gentle and it felt good. He let me go and turned me around to face my door.

"I'll see you on Tuesday night at seven," he whispered.

I nodded.

"Go ahead."

I ran in as fast as I could and peeled my soaked panties off just as soon as the door closed behind me.

We shared dinner on two more occasions and I stayed away from my favorite bar stool. I wasn't quite ready to play his game again, but dinner was safe. He was always mild mannered when we went out and would listen to me chatter on about anything as he smiled or laughed at my anecdotes about work and my family. But on our fourth date he watched me quietly.

I knew instantly that he was restless, though he hardly moved in his chair nor was there a flicker of impatience in his voice. It was obvious from the portentous look in his eyes as he stared at me across the table. I had looked up the meaning of his name (along with his zodiac sign) and I tried to lighten the atmosphere by teasing him as his gaze bored into me over a salad.

"So, are you powerful?"

"Only if you want me to be."

He didn't smile back and I looked away as I thought about that. *Did I want him to be?*

He waited for me to get most of the way through my salad before he signaled for the check. He held my hand during the ten minute cab ride. I couldn't look away from the warm feeling of my hand swallowed within his. He was completely confident that I was okay with where we were going. His place. He was right. I wanted him to be as powerful as I could stand it, and in every way he could imagine.

His bedroom was dimly lit by two small lamps in the far corners. The bed was huge and made up with dark cotton sheets.

"Be still," he told me as I stood before him.

His fingers looked blunt and clumsy, but were surprisingly nimble and adept at undressing me. He knelt. It took every ounce of will power I had not to step back as he took off my pumps, reached behind me to unzip my skirt. I shivered as it fell to the floor. The room was warm -- very warm -- but goose bumps riddled my body as his fingers whispered against me when he unbuttoned my blouse. Another mind-numbing shiver rattled me as his lips brushed across my lower belly.

I thought I was prepared for him. I had on a new pair of lace panties, held up with tiny bows that I had carefully tied over each hip. Above, I wore a pearlescent bra that barely held my heaving breasts in check. He unclasped it in a nanosecond and I *swear* my boobs had never sprung forward like that before.

I closed my eyes when the top of his head leaned toward me. He planted a gentle kiss on both of my thighs.

"You're beautiful," he murmured.

My heart was pounding, I was so desperate to feel him inside me. But he bade me be still. And still I was.

Until he stood up and pulled a black silk scarf out of his pocket.

I gasped and backed up. I shook my head as I looked up at him, silently pleading with him not to. But with a hand at my back he prevented me from moving any further. He was either ignoring me or didn't notice my distress as he leaned forward and covered my eyes.

"Your hands are still free," he told me as he gently tied the scarf over my hair. "For the moment."

He kissed me slowly as he cupped the back of my head and I melted around his invading tongue. Sensations of urgency blossomed behind my eyes as his tongue swirled over mine and we tasted each other for the first time. His fingers freed the bowties on each side of my panties, they fell to the floor. My coochie throbbed in unison with my heart.

The edge of the bed pressed against the back of my thighs and he lifted me up and sat me down on it. When he left me I couldn't stop my chin from rising as my lips parted, blindly searching for him. I could hear him getting undressed: the sound of his shoes landing on the floor, followed by the tantalizing purr of his zipper sliding down. I gripped the edge of the mattress as my feet dangled in midair.

He pressed his hands against my thighs and spread them wide. Even though I was wet and swollen with anticipation, I jumped again. Because I didn't see it coming.

"Did you do this for me?" he asked.

His breath whispered against my ear and my body hummed under his fingers as he traced them over bare skin that I'd had waxed earlier that day. Just a thin strip of hair remained over my pubis; my labia was as smooth as an egg. It was incredibly painful when it happened, but I had known what to expect then. I had been warned before the process. At the time I could look down and brace myself for it. But there was no warning from him. I moaned and trembled as he rubbed his thumb over my naked sex.

"Y-yes."

"Good. I'm gonna enjoy sucking you."

I relaxed as his hand moved to my lower back and pulled me forward, all the way to the edge of the bed, but my nerves jumped back into high gear when he gathered my wrists behind me and held them together within one of his own.

"Red light means stop," he said.

I nodded, though I didn't really get it. All I knew was that his hand was holding both of mine behind me, I was completely naked, and completely blind. I couldn't see a red light. But I nodded anyway. All rational thought went on hiatus as the primal animal I had become screamed *NOW!*

Still, I was held captive by a huge hand and a massive body in front of me.

"This doesn't work without trust." he said.

I nodded.

"It's early for us, but I need you–" he kissed my throat and I sighed under those wonderful lips. "To trust me."

I bit my lip as he continued.

"And for that you need a safe word in case I go further than you're willing. So when you say 'red light' it means you want me to stop."

"Okay," I whispered.

I felt him lean in and I trembled as a warm hand clasped a cold manacle over my left ankle. The cuff was attached to something that felt like bungee cord, which immediately pulled my leg taut against the bed frame. Even though I knew it was coming, I couldn't believe that I wasn't screaming "RED LIGHT!" when he put the matching shackle on. My breath came and went a little faster as my legs were held wide open. There was no denying that I was as wet as a dripping faucet by the time my right leg was pulled back.

"You asked me once why I think we're compatible," Edric said. "It's because your lovely face and this beautiful body called to me."

I held my breath for a few seconds as his fingers traced a line along the inside of my knee.

"I knew as soon as I saw you, you'd be perfect. Right here. Just as you are."

He used his hand behind me to pull me forward. I felt exposed as his fingers crept up my leg. My heart boomed and stuttered in my chest. Images flitted behind my eyes with camera-shutter speed: my body arched with my hands between my legs, Edric's smoky dark eyes, his lips on my skin, his fingers caressing my midriff. I turned away and bit my lip as a whimper escaped me.

His fingers slowly snaked up the inside of my thigh as I sat there, legs spread and tied open for his enjoyment.

My trepidation was so complete, it bordered on fear. Yet it was all so *ferociously* exciting, I couldn't help but surrender to it. His fingers found the very center of me and I moaned as they slid inside. I gasped repeatedly as he probed and explored me while his tongue licked my upper lip and tasted the corners of my mouth. I breathed like someone who had just won a marathon.

"Don't move." He left me again. I listened as he moved around the bed until it shifted under his weight behind me.

Smooth silk pressed against my wrists as he tied them gently together at my lower back. I tensed up, though my hands were loosely bound and I wasn't uncomfortable. He whispered in my ear.

"I want you to give in to every thrill that comes over you. I don't want your hands or your eyes, or any part of you, to interrupt the way you feel."

I nodded silently, though my body tensed and trembled and tensed again. A sense of urgency and impatience rattled my bones and backlit my mind as I felt him in front of me once more. I held my breath to keep from hyperventilating.

"Are you scared?"

His voice, deep and seductive below my ear, was muffled against my throat as he cupped the back of my head and tilted my chin to the ceiling.

Slippery heat trickled between my legs as my body acknowledged that I could do nothing to escape whatever he did to me after that moment. Except for the red light.

"You can tell me," he whispered, and kissed the underside of my breast.

I moaned as his lips fastened over my nipple. He licked then blew a cool breath over my taut skin. My nipples had never been that erect in all my life – they simply *throbbed* under his mouth.

"I…" I bit my lip and squeezed my eyes shut beneath the blindfold and shook my head in his hand. I couldn't stop shaking, I couldn't stop the hesitant way I was breathing. I couldn't stop the slick fire between my thighs from trickling down onto his sheets. I whimpered and trembled uncontrollably as his fingers slid inside me and he arched my body. I couldn't stop anything, that much I could admit to. "I can't."

"The sound of you…" Edric's voice blew gently against my other nipple and between short breaths I moaned shamelessly. "Is such a turn on…"

He laid me down and the pressure of my hands behind me forced me to arch my back as his lips traced their way down my belly, over my thighs, and between my legs. I loved the superlatively torturous way he licked me from the bottom of my naked inner cheeks to the tip of my clit.

"Ooooh...." I pressed closer as his lips inspired trills of pleasure. I gripped the sheets beneath my hands when he stuck his tongue inside me; stars winked at me from an atmosphere I had never glimpsed before. I could hear a vibrator in the distance and held my breath once more as he rubbed it against my thigh.

"I bought this for you," he murmured against me. "The day after we met."

I was swept into in a continuing vortex of pleasure that was as tumultuous as the rose of Saturn.

The thought that he had been bold enough to buy a vibrator for me weeks before we were naked with each other, never crossed my mind. At least not until later, when he admitted he had fantasized about me as much as I had about him. I savored the first of many orgasm-inducing gifts.

"Mmmm...." I became ecstatic as he moved the vibrator closer and closer to my sweetly soaked labia. "Yes…" I moaned and lifted my hips. "Please…"

I sighed with sincere gratitude as he slid it inside me and it hummed against my g-spot. He licked and sucked my tiny star and just as the ocean is helpless against the hypnotic call of the moon, my waters surged and rushed forward until my body went supernova.

I was panting from exhaustion when I felt his knees beside mine and he reached behind me to untie my hands.

"There's more than one way to experience bondage" Edric murmured against my mouth as my hand searched between us. I gripped him and wasn't surprised by his size, but at how hard he was. My hips arched with needful intent as I squeezed and rubbed my thumb over the condom and helped his pre-cum coat the tip of his dick. I was satisfied to hear him groan in my ear.

"But for someone as small as you," he whispered, "it's easy."

I gasped again when he pulled my hands together above my head and held them within one of his own. Incredibly, there was plenty of give to the ties around my ankles and with one strong hand beneath my knee he lifted my leg over his forearm and slid inside me.

"Oooh!" I cried out as my body arched up to him.

"Oh, shit you're tight," he groaned as his hand pressed me closer.

I could feel his heart pounding above my ear as he moved slowly against me. I whimpered as he filled me with a covetous presence that I never knew was possible. He nuzzled my cheek with his nose and talked me through the slowest and sexiest grind of my life.

"No fear..." he whispered as I gripped his hands. "You feel so good...I don't want you to have any fear..." I gasped as his teeth nipped my shoulder. "I'll be good to you..." He pressed deeper inside me. "Trust me...give yourself to me..."

My entire body shook and even my lips trembled as we kissed and he moved faster, all the while whispering erogenous words between each determined and delectable stroke. I squeezed my eyes tighter as his voice poured into my ears and his thunder rolled between my thighs.

"Give me..." He pressed an expansive hand against my lower back and pulled my hips up as he slid out but came back stronger. I shivered as he growled like a hungry bear. "All of you..."

I gave him more than I knew I had, and he made me come over and over again while I cried out, panted, gasped, and whimpered repeatedly as he kissed me, held my hands captive and fucked me senseless.

Throughout the night I gave in to every stroke, reaching higher heights of star studded ecstasy, as he took me, blind and bound, beyond our atmosphere.

It's been six months since my first trip to the cosmos behind my eyes.

In the evenings, Edric takes me dancing, out to dinner and frequently to the movies. I discovered that he loves to laugh and enjoys kissing my hands as soon as he sees me. By now I fall asleep most nights gathered close against him.

But I never forgot what he told me that first night we were together. That I was perfect as I sat tied open before him. And even though I still get nervous and shaky every time he tells me to be still, I was finally able to admit to him one night in a whisper in the dark, that I love it.

For Mikki, Marion, Jacquette, Earline
AND
Khali Hammond

Belly Button

Lately I find myself tense with a gripping expectation I can't explain. It's there and I can't ignore it. I watch the clock knowing that in five minutes I'll make my call and say what I've been saying at the end of every work day and without warning on the weekends. She'll answer the same, with a familiar but new voice. Experienced but with youthful anxiety. I'm compelled to be early, three minutes ahead of the schedule I've kept for a month now and will likely keep forever.

I loosen my tie and press the second button on the phone at my desk. We play the game on cue, neither of us says hello.

"Are you ready?"

"Yes."

Modern technology makes personal the timid excitement in her whisper. Instantly I'm as hard as a brick, as the gentle sound waves of lusty promise caress first my ear then my loins with an invisible hand that strokes my shaft. I stand up as my dick stands up.

"I'm on my way."

I shouldn't be surprised that my hair feels electrified the way it did the first time I asked her that question. It was the afternoon of my greatest discovery. How had I missed it for ten years? But it's too late in the day for musings.

Rigidity forces me to take my time as I close my up desk. I turn off the computer, click off the overhead lights, the desk lamp that held the dreary grey day at bay and think about mundane things. Images of meetings and the next day's demands finally allow me to leave my office with a flat pair of slacks and a modicum of dignity. I see but ignore the warm, slow smiles of the women I pass in the hall or stand next to in the elevator, and the openly flirtatious look of the new exec on third floor as she stands next to me in line in the parking garage. The word in the board room is that she's ready for whatever is required to advance her status. Supposedly I'm to be checked off as first on her list. Being CEO has its privileges. Little does she know I could care less. Its 5:10 and I have better things to do.

The sensual sounds of Robert Glasper's *Ah Yeah* banishes the frustration of a long rainy day commute on 76 West. My tie rests beside me in a leather messenger. The top buttons of my Egyptian cotton oxford are undone by the time I pull into the car port. The bag stays in the car. Home is no place for work.

On my way up I stop in the kitchen to pour a glass of wine. Hers is beside her already, this I know. With my jacket over one arm and the other hand working off the rest of my shirt, I take a few seconds and think about last night's confessions.

"It's because I've lost a little weight, isn't it?" she asked.

"No."

It's not entirely a lie. There is some truth to the way the shed pounds have allowed her to lose inhibitions I never noticed she had. It freed her hands to lay beside her, helped spread her legs wide with a lack of humility. I love everything about her and always have. But it was probably modesty that hid who she really is.

My wife is still a voluptuous woman. Neither tall nor short, fat nor skinny, but heavily shaped and completely seductive. I can't tell if it was the roll of her hips, the promise of overpowering consummation between her firm thighs or the provocative sound of her richly spiced laughter that reminded me of the first time I had Dominican *Café*. I was amazed and instantly hooked.

Whatever *it* was, she held me captive from the first moment I saw her at a cocktail party almost twelve years ago. I knew instantly that I had to come home to her. I was born to cup her ample bottom in my hands and bury my face against breasts softer than the finest silk. I was made to lose myself in the treasures of her abundance for the rest of my days. I was *sprung* like a twelve year-old after his first ejaculation. We were married within two years and I've watched her hips sway to a hypnotic rhythm all their own ever since. But she's different now.

I so enjoy my contemporary wife, the one who is willing to try anything that pops into either of our heads at a moment's notice. It's her I rush home to, this woman of odalisque ways that leads me forever onward toward new lewd and libertine desires. My wife of long gowns and soft discoveries beneath, is gone forever.

Lately a light bulb has come on, a new scent has wafted to my nose, or perhaps my eyes are wide open. I'm like an alcoholic at the bar. I reach for her in the darkness of morning and become eager toward the close of business. I can't even think about anything else after I shut my office door.

My belt is off, my shoes just make it to the top of the riser before they're discarded and I turn the corner at the top of the stairs to see her sitting on the bed. Waiting for me.

"Aaahh…"

With a smile on her lips she puts the wine glass on the nightstand beside her as I discard my slacks. She's wearing the teddy I bought at lunch time. Home delivery is a beautiful thing and I've been waiting for this all day.

"Lie down."

I'm dying to see the pink crotchless panties reveal the juiciest treasure on earth. I strip completely as she lies back on the bed. As always her knees are pressed together, because I haven't said otherwise.

"Open your legs."

I spend a few minutes caressing the inside of her thighs with patient fingers before I relieve her of the lacy panties. Only the top half of my noon purchase remains to hide her breasts and my most coveted prize. But first things first.

I pull my short chair in front of the bed and smile as I gently finger the soft skin at the bottom of her ass as it peeks out just enough for me to pinch and lick. I don't disappoint and listen as she sighs softly.

I love my chair. I searched high and low for two weeks in furniture and antique stores for miles around before I finally found it in an adult toy store downtown. It's the perfect height for a man my size, just right for me to sit in as my fingers and mouth explore the moist flower between her thighs.

The house is quiet, just the way I like it. I want to hear every moan, every salacious groan, every wet drop drip and coat my fingers before I dive in. First is my finger in her rectum. She knows it is coming but it shocks her every time. I remember the first time I did it, almost a month ago. I couldn't say why even then, but again, I was compelled. Her muscles close around my finger and I think back to the time after when she told me she liked it and didn't like it. She couldn't explain and I never stopped. She inhales sharply and her hips rise up a little in response to the intrusion. With an arm beneath her knees I lift her hips completely to reveal an ass juicier than the ripest mango. I press my nose between her cheeks.

"Mmmm...."

I inhale her sweet, invigorating smell and love it. I can't help tasting and licking around my finger as it moves further in and slides back out. My tongue coats the fine hairs below and leads my taste buds to the first ripe drops of passion at the borders of her vagina. She breathes harder and begins to tremble. I'm in heaven as I spread her before me.

It's crucial that I take my time and miss no part of her smooth brown thighs, not a centimeter of her luscious labia. I must suck and pull and drink what's inside her as a thirsty man will guzzle water from the heart of a cactus in the center of the desert.

I'm duty-bound to stick my tongue inside her as far as it will go and imitate the thrusts of my manhood to come. I'm thrilled and excited as she moans above me, I oblige her when she cries out as I lick the tip of her clit before I pull it further into the cave of my mouth and stroke it lovingly with my tongue.

My finger wishes not to be forgotten and is joined with his longer brother inside her as thick, sweet nectar drips down around them. They are obligated to thrust deeper, go further, and they do so of their own free will, as my tongue caresses above.

"YES!"

She screams out as she cups the back of my head and instinctively tries to hide from the brothers' exploration. But there is not a hip lift in the world that can escape them and they renew their intercourse vigorously as she breathlessly pushes the sweet flower against my lips. It's the thrust I've been waiting for.

My tongue takes its cue from the firmness beneath it and clasps her with an intensity that is almost violent. Her clit is as hard as my dick and I suck her with a ferocity that I cannot abate.

"Oh! Ohohohoh...yes!...please...make me come, please!"

The sound of her breathless moaning just about sets my hair on fire and I give her what she needs until she spills into my mouth with a shuddering groan. I drink and drink and drink of her until she begs me to stop.

She sits up as I stand so she can take me in.

Sliding my dick into the warm moisture of her mouth should be the highlight of my day. It's true, my eyes roll back and I can't restrain the groan of satisfaction as her tongue swirls around the head and laps up the first drops of my approval.

Her fingers first whisper against my balls before they grip them firmly and pull as her mouth pushes down into my crotch. She gives the best brain I've ever had. Even her nails, gripping my butt cheeks as her lips suck the tight skin of my shaft, are mind-bending. She keeps it wet, pulls gently but firmly, swirls her tongue teasingly over me without pulling out and sucks my dick with a joy I'll never understand. I can feel my balls tightening as my phallus jumps and bounces against the back of her throat. If I don't stop her I'll choke her to death with a geyser of sperm.

In the nick of time I push her onto her back and shove myself inside her before it's too late. She cries out, but is as still as I am as we wait for it to pass.

"Oh, love…" I whisper as my dick throbs, pulses and stretches. "Oh, my beautiful love…"

Another second cannot be wasted within the tightest walls of my life. She feels as new as a virgin, grips me on all sides, squeezes instinctively on every front and tickles my helmet with an upward thrust.

Our bodies are slick with sweat, as our thick and heavy sex extract creates smacking sounds between us, our stomachs clash against one another and our pelvises pull back and plunge in repeatedly. I'm moaning heavily as she holds me with silken thighs around my waist while the onslaught of a powerful momentum propels us into a satisfaction-seeking sexual congress that is matchless.

I can feel her nails digging into my back, raking new lines across the ones from this morning, yet I cannot stop. I can hear her breathing harder, feel her stretching beneath me as my dick swells to the point of cracking the protective skin around it. With one last savage thrust, I'm spewing inside her. I kiss her face as she smiles at me and my hips spurt forward and give up the last few drops. It's so damn good I want to do it all over again.

I nuzzle her neck and lick tasty drops of sweat. I dip my mouth lower as my hand pushes aside the gauzy lace to find each nipple, as tender and succulent as they were this morning. There is no milk, yet I lick and pull on them with them the eagerness of a hungry baby just the same. I go lower still to find my prize.

Nestled in the middle of her waist, above her lovely curving hips, is the prettiest, sweetest belly button I've ever come to know. I can't help the reverent kisses I shower on my grandest discovery about my wife. It's an outtie with the characteristics of an innie, there but just barely seen, surrounded by the softest skin a body could have.

She knows what I want. She hands me her wine glass.

"Thank you."

I adore this part of our love making almost as much as I crave coming inside the tight warmth of her sticky haven.

I pour just one drop in the well. Zealously I suck out the sweet sangria mixed with the honey drizzle that is the essence of her skin, with lascivious joy.

I pour in another drop and suck it out, and another and another, until I'm almost drunk with delight.

"You really like that little thing, don't you?" she asks with a grin.

"More than you know."

The O Spa

Prologue

I thought Philly would be my new beginning. When I left Arizona, I promised myself that I would never again have to look over my shoulder. I intended to live in a city where no one had ever heard of me, let alone seen my mug shot. This city was going to be the place where I eked out a happy existence. But sometimes shit happens while you're making other plans.

My footfalls echoed on the hardwood floor as I ran around and collected a few things. I walked out, locked my door and took the stairs to the ground floor. I stopped in front of my mailbox and wondered if I was making the right choice. I had worked hard at rebuilding my life. Watching it all circle the drain over the last few days had been so stressful that I hadn't really taken the time to sort out how I felt. Nervous. But then, being nervous had never prevented me from being seduced and loving it.

I smoothed down my silk blouse and made a quick left to the side door. The car at the end of Sansom Street was waiting to take me someplace I never imagined I'd go.

First Trip

"Just try it, Sydney." Cheryl put her hands on my shoulders. "I promise you won't be disappointed. You look stressed out. I bet the new position is making matters worse."

I turned away and reached for the coffeepot. "Cheryl, I don't have time for a day spa, let alone a week someplace." She stood beside me in the break room while I poured my third cup of the day.

"Look, you haven't taken a vacation in almost two years! Didn't John recommend some time off before the next quarter starts?"

"Yeah, he did. But I have to clean out my in-box, make a client list for Susan before she moves up here, be sure that Michael—"

"Stop!" Cheryl held up her hand. "Just wait a minute."

I let her take the coffee cup out of my hand, but I decided right then and there that I would still say no. Cheryl was my only true friend since I had moved to Philly just three years ago. She usually had my best interests at heart. Even when her idea of my best interests was a little skewed from my own. She held my hand and patted it twice. A clear sign that some supreme bullshit was coming my way.

"Listen. They have great massages there. They have gourmet meals, hot tubs and huge showers, a full kitchen, an array of televisions and stereos with MP3 attachments, thick fuzzy bathrobes, and all the green tea you can stand." She looked me in the eye before her final pitch. "I presented that certificate to you on Christmas

Day and it's March already. It's gonna expire soon. I'm begging you. Please go. Just try it for a day and if you don't like it—"

"Cheryl, I—"

"If you don't like it after twenty-four hours, you can call me and I'll make arrangements to pick up the rest of your days."

"Cheryl. I simply don't have time. You'll have to take the whole seven days yourself." I watched her eyes slide to the left as her shoulders drooped a little.

"I've already put in your vacation request and John approved it yesterday."

"WHAAAAT?"

She nodded slowly in spite of the fact that my hand had hers in a vise grip. "Yeah," she whispered. "I did."

"I can't believe you!" I snatched my hand back.

"Syd, just—"

"Syd, my ass! Who do you think you are? Are you trying to undermine me? Make me look incompetent?"

"Sydney, it's Friday and it's almost six in the evening. We're the only ones in our department still here. You're the only one who got a long-awaited raise and a promotion this year." She sighed. "Nobody deserves it more than you, but I gotta be honest and tell you that at the age of thirty-two, you're also the only one—"

"Lemme tell you some—"

"In our department on the fast track to a heart attack."

I felt like she gave me a gut-buster. I couldn't breathe. It wasn't her fault, though. She didn't know that I had come a little over twenty-three hundred miles so I could start over. She didn't know how hard I had to work for two years, just to reaffirm myself to the woman in the mirror as well as to my peers. I threw myself into my work because I had to.

I caught myself rubbing my wrists against each other and forced my hands to my sides, glad that I was able to. All Cheryl knew was that I had relocated for this job and my only living relative was my mom, retired in Connecticut, living the life of a content but lonely widow. I had left out a lot of events in my life as we got to know each other. Especially the fact that ten years prior, at age fifty-seven, my father had died of a massive coronary blowout.

"Sydney."

I wondered if she could see the shock and hurt on my face, 'cause I damn sure felt it.

"I want you to enjoy yourself for a little while," Cheryl went on. "Be able to relax, and release all the stress and worry that you carry around with you every day." She gave me the cute puppy look. "I didn't mean to hurt you or make you look incompetent. I just want you to take a break. You deserve it. I love you and I want you to be happy." She smiled. "Like I am."

"Damn." I thought about my dad, the workaholic. "Okay." I nodded slowly. "I'll go."

"Good!" Cheryl clapped her hands. "I've already mapped the directions from your house and I have them in my phone!"

"Just give me the address." I really wanted that cup of coffee so I could tackle the files on my desk. How relaxed was I going to be drinking green tea in a fluffy robe with all that work on my mind? "I'll send it to my navigation system."

Cheryl had this quickstep way of walking when she was onto something she called 'hot.' I watched her do a slow version of a New Orleans Second Line step down the hall while she chattered like a morning bird. I wondered if she even heard anything I said after I agreed to go. I shook my head and felt sorry for the unsuspecting man who would one day marry her. She always seemed to get her way.

True to form, she whisked me out of my office like a tornado in progress, mouth running a mile a minute. She actually rode behind me in her car, talking energetically through my headset on the way to my spot, and ran her mouth like a pro at freestyle rap concert while she helped me get outta there.

I did notice the way she looked at the clothes I packed. What I *didn't* notice right away were the Christmas gifts she bought me, all of them stashed in the netted zipper part of my luggage.

Had I been paying attention to what she was doing and not to what she was saying, I would've unpacked the three sweat suits and the two yoga outfits that I threw in with my cross trainers, and asked her what the hell was going on. But she was yapping her head off, the way she does when she's excited or happy or both, and I was preoccupied by it, as usual. I later learned that distraction goes a long way in a subterfuge.

Before I could catch my breath and make sure that I had my damn *toothbrush* packed, I was locking up and running behind her as she rolled my bag to my car and promptly dumped it in the trunk.

"Okay!" Cheryl smiled. "Call me if you cut your time short so I can transfer your days over to my account."

"I will." I remember thinking that she was the one who needed to lay off the coffee. "Thanks again, Cheryl. I'll call you and let you know how it's going."

She gave me another funny look. "You can if you want to."

I smiled, hugged her, and assured her that I had the address in my GPS. She told me not to think of anything but relaxation, and she jumped in her car, honking as she went her own way.

It turned out that she was right. I didn't even think of—let alone attempt—to call her and let her know how things were going while I was there. As a matter of fact, when I finally did get home, I called her a stinking cow and threatened to black her eye.

But by then, what was done could not be undone.

Sydney

Once I drove almost an hour beyond the city limits, the world became as dark as outer space. The distant lights of homes and chintzy strip malls fell away until there was only my headlights and the persistent *coc coc* sound of the ruts beneath my tires to remind me I was still on earth. The Pennsylvania Turnpike wound up and down amid frequent curves. The change in atmosphere clogged then popped my ears as my car climbed and dipped down the many hills beyond the Lehigh Tunnel.

Even with music playing and the verbal reminder to 'keep on this course' from the virtual directions map, the drive was long and tiresome. Especially after a busy workday. Within an hour, I found myself looking forward to a warm, cozy evening in one of those fluffy robes Cheryl had bragged about. Full wine glass included.

After two hours of listening to jazz and following my headlights on the dark and foggy road, I finally reached my exit. I paid my fare and followed the navigation's verbal cue to make a right at the end of the ramp. Four miles beyond the exit, I made another right onto a newly paved road that led me down a sparsely lit path, until I reached a polished stone wall that rose higher than I could crane my neck up to see over.

In the middle of the wall was a black metal gate. Beside the gate was a small callbox. I pressed the glowing red button and a female voice answered.

"How may I serve you?"

"Uhh…hi. My name is Sydney Cooper and I have a reservation."

"Oh yes, Miss Cooper. Welcome to The OSpa. We've been expecting you." The voice paused and I heard paper rattling. "Please drive through the gate, make the first available left turn and proceed to cottage number nine."

The gate opened like a creepy castle entrance. "Thank you."

"May all your dreams come true."

I looked at the box and remembered that was the motto on the small gift card that Cheryl gave me last year. "After driving over the hills and through the woods, I certainly hope so."

The first available left led me onto a lane flanked with tall, thick bushes on both sides. An immediate sense of claustrophobia caused me to grip the steering wheel but the dense hedges soon gave way and spread out twenty feet to flank a lush lawn and stone pavers to the front door. The bushes were like privacy gates that towered as tall as the roof.

By the time I got my traveler out of the trunk, I noticed lights twinkling in the distance between the bushes and decided that a little solitude might be a good thing. I'm not a fan of small talk with strangers.

My cottage already had a few lights on inside. I stopped at the brass mailbox beside the front door. In spite of my earlier misgivings, the whole joint looked like a nice getaway. A home away from home, so to speak, and I got excited at the thought of a warm soak.

In the mailbox was a large envelope with my name across the front in script letters. I thought it was a list of all the mud scrubs and salad menus. I got halfway to the door and realized that check-in was a little odd. I went back to the mailbox again. Just off to the side was a little slot on the wall of the box with a key in it. I stood just inside the doorway, smiling.

"Veeerrrry nice!"

Just beyond the spring colors on the doormat was a spacious living room with gunmetal-colored walls, the alcoves and trim a lighter shade of slate. Above the hardwood floor was a white chaise lounge opposite a white, deep-seated sofa. Between the two sitting pieces was a long teak-wood table. Opposite the sitting area was a massive teak entertainment center, resplendent with double doors in the middle and drawers below. Its glass doors were warmed with low interior lights above the decorative crystal goblets and snifters.

I took in the contemporary look of the room and was surprised that I even liked the artwork sprinkled in discrete places, the soothing colors of silver, and deep burnished wood mixed in with brown and gray glass lamps.

Farther in was a formal dining room. An oval table covered with a silver lace-trimmed tablecloth was set with bone china, shining flatware, champagne flutes, wine goblets, and brandy snifters. I ran my finger along the edge of a white leather dining chair.

A few feet beyond the dining room was a galley kitchen. White marble dripped down the walls beneath the cabinets to become countertops that contrasted wonderfully with sleek appliances. Reflections of the stainless steel built-in refrigerator and professional stove beside the dishwasher, the built-in microwave, and coffee/espresso center gleamed in the polished hardwood hardwood floor. I liked what I saw, although the only things I planned on using in there were the ice machine and the coffee center. In my opinion, the only thing ever worth leaving home for was room service.

I turned around toward the hall and my shoes sank into the carpet. I almost felt bad dragging my rolling suitcase behind me. The hallway beyond the dining room led me to three doors on the right and a double set centered at the back.

The first door on the right opened into a large shower room with a double sink and built-in cabinets, one of which held an MP3 speaker dock. Waist-to-ceiling mirrors covered the walls on one side of the room. In their reflection I could see the huge shower stall behind me.

I went to the next door in the hall and discovered a tub room that was just as large as the first. The tub room was the color of blue tropical water, but what bowled me over was the size of the tub. It looked like it could hold five people comfortably, and although it had all the faucets of a traditional tub, on the immediate right ledge were a multitude of power buttons for the air jets. Waterproof pillows adhered strategically above each built-in seat.

Behind the third door were two thrones. Looking back, I can laugh at myself, but at the time I had no idea why there would be two toilets in the same room, nor why one of them had a chain beside it. Actually, I thought it was a little elegant, so I left my bag in the hall and sat on the one beside the pretty silver chain. I got the surprise of my life when I pulled it and warm water splashed up to tickle my coochie!

"Oh my God!" I shot up off the toilet and realized I'd had my first bidet experience. I laughed for a whole minute before I had a sneaky thought, and stuck my booty out for a little more. The water tickle was nice, and I immediately wished I had remembered my vibrator.

The bedroom was equally elegant. It held the tallest and widest king-sized bed I'd ever seen—I'd find out later it was called a California King—made up with the softest white linens atop a mattress that was simply dreamy. I hoisted my modest traveler on it and quickly unpacked my clothes in the armoire, pulled back the covers, unpacked my favorite book, and strategically placed the remote for the flat screen opposite the huge four poster so I could watch a little TV if I wanted before sleep.

But first, other matters had to be tended to.

After a long, hot shower, I dried off and took just a few minutes to blow dry my hair. I knew everyone at the job thought I cut it all off after being hit on repeatedly—ok, maybe that did have something to do with it—but the truth was that living in Philly gave me a different perspective on being a black woman. My newly adopted home has a theory that a sista's hair can be styled in any way that pleases her and she's still beautiful. Every day for weeks, I saw so many women who looked like me—fair skinned, hippy and a little thick in some places—with short hair! I cut my curly 'do down to a Peter Pan coif and have been happy with my new look ever since. Satisfied that I didn't need gel or mouse to watch TV, I wrapped myself in a fluffy white robe that hugged and soothed me from my neck to my feet. I walked into the living room and poured myself a glass of Merlot from a bottle I'd found in the armoire. I took a sip, sat down on the chaise and opened the envelope from my mailbox.

PLEASE CALL ME BEFORE READING. Tabitha ext. 000.

I shrugged and walked over to the small workstation on the other side of the room and used the cordless.

"Hello, Miss Cooper," a breathy female answered on the second ring.

"Hello. Is this Tabitha?"

"Yes, it is. I gather you're ready for your first meeting."

"What kind of meeting do you mean? I'm actually ready for bed."

"You couldn't have picked a better time. Don't bother to get dressed or anything like that. I'll be there in less than five minutes."

"For what?"

"I'm coming over to explain the options in your gift packet to ensure that you enjoy all that The OSpa has to offer. We want to make all your dreams come true and we can't do that unless we know what you like."

"Well…"

"It'll only take a few minutes and then you can take some time to peruse our exciting menu and select the type of services that suit you."

"Alright then, I'll see you shortly."

I hung up the phone and took a sip of wine, determined not to let anything interrupt my already-cozy feeling. Within five minutes the doorbell rang and I pulled the collar of my robe a little closer before I answered it.

Tabitha looked just the way she sounded: petite, blonde-haired, blue-eyed, probably size zero, youngish-looking woman in a tight blue pinstriped miniskirt suit and high heels. In spite of her windswept hairdo, her abundant cleavage bursting out of the vee of her jacket and the half-inch of makeup covering her face, she smiled at me in a friendly fashion. Tucked under one arm was a leather-bound portfolio.

"Hello, Miss Cooper, and welcome to OSpa!" She held out her hand.

"Thank you!" I smiled back, gave her a quick shake. "Please come in."

She sat down on the couch.

"I see you're already settled in, so I'll make this as quick as I can."

I hoped she truly could. I was in no mood to hear a sales pitch for a vacation club or some crap.

"Here at OSpa, we strive to fulfill your every fantasy, your every wish, and every desire, which we hope will make your dreams comes true."

"Wait a minute. What do you mean, fantasy?"

"Fantasies," Tabitha answered matter-of-factly. "Sexual desires."

I blinked. "Sexual?"

"Yes, your sexual fantasies."

"Hold it." I held one hand up. "I thought this was a spa. Like massages and yoga and green tea?"

"Miss Cooper." Tabitha gave me a sincere look. "The O in OSpa stands for orgasm."

"WHAAAT???" My shock came out in a panicky screech. It's a wonder Tabitha didn't just fall back hee-hawing all over herself.

What she did do was add to my astonishment by pulling a doobie out of her cleavage. From somewhere else in the nether regions of her skirt came a lighter.

"Do you mind if I smoke?" she asked.

I shook my head and Tabitha lit up, filling the room with the sweet head-spinning aroma of marijuana.

"Okay." She flipped open her leather book. "It says here that you've been enrolled for a one-month trial membership, and as a gift you've been given the seven day bonus package. By the way." She blew smoke out of her nose. "This cottage has three wet bars. One in here, one in your bedroom and a mini-bar in the tub room. Each room is also equipped with three ashtrays and two bongs."

I watched her stand up and walk over to the entertainment center, flip down the top door to reveal a second fully stocked bar with liquors of every taste and variety, surrounded by an array of glasses, snifters, and crystal decanters.

Wow was all I could think as I watched her reach for a large ashtray on the shelf below the glasses. I'm pretty sure my mouth was hanging open.

"You are free to use your choice of drugs, and most of the guests that you invite can bring you a bag of weed or some X at your request."

Tabitha sat down opposite me again with the ashtray and the joint in the middle of us on the coffee table.

"G-guests?" I stammered.

"Yes, I'll get to that in a minute."

She offered me the joint. "No thanks." I picked up my glass and took a gulp.

"It also says here that your friend admits that you know nothing of this spa and that you are not well acquainted with your pussy."

I choked on my wine.

"Oh!" Tabitha jumped up as I sputtered and wine ran down my chin. "Are you alright?"

I coughed and wheezed, but held my hand up. "I'm…" I coughed hard one more time. "I'm okay." I took a deep breath. "Wha-what did she say?"

"She says you're not well acquainted with your pussy and she recommends that you meet with a tailor before engaging in any sexual activity."

"What? Can I see that?"

Tabitha handed over the binder and when I inspected the document I was shocked. It looked like a professional contract, but the heading was different. The spa title read *Discreet Decompression: Golf and Relaxation Spa.* I found my name and address, a checked box next to the words *New Guest.* Below that was a gift allocation of seven days to sample all services available, and just below all that were the letters *WHIFF.*

"What is this whiff business?" I asked.

"WHIFF is when a golfer swings and misses," Tabitha said. "But we use it as a code word for a woman who doesn't know her own body. Particularly her vagina."

"Okay." I handed over the portfolio and stood up. "You can leave now. 'Cause I'm gonna be right behind you."

"Miss Cooper." Tabitha calmly took another toke and looked at me through the smoky haze. "Have you ever considered what it would feel like to have multiple orgasms, day after day, in the most delightful positions you can imagine?"

That comment stopped me in my tracks.

"Just think for a minute," she said. "You can be shy or aggressive, get a full body massage—and I do mean full body—from as many hands as you can stand at the same time, and at the end of all that, allow someone to suck and fuck your G-spot until you either explode or you can't take another second. You can dress up or stay naked. You can be anyone you choose. You can give your pussy away or have someone come in and take it roughly. You can play any and every game you can think of, or just get fucked until you don't want to anymore. Whatever you like."

I sat back down.

"You can lie back and let your guests do all the work, or participate completely," she went on. "With a man or a woman or both. You can come in whatever way pleases you. Repeatedly. As this is a private spa with rigorous guidelines for membership, our staff adheres to the strictest rules of confidentiality. No one will know."

I took the bone when she offered it the second time. I pulled in deep while she looked down at the page in front of her.

"You've already been signed up for the maximum of five guests and a fitting with your tailor."

She watched me to gauge my reaction but I was stupefied. A sex spa. Was anything sacred?

I took another toke and suddenly realized that I hadn't had sex since almost a month before my horrifying breakup with Frank. The weed started to cloud my mind and probably my better judgment when I realized that I hadn't had *good* and *fulfilling* sex in I don't know how long. *Fuck it.* I pulled hard on the best weed—really the only weed—I'd had in a long time. *Maybe one good round with a pro might not be such a bad idea.*

"Okay." I passed it back. "What is this guest thing? I came by myself."

She smiled. "A guest is really a staff member. But as you invite them into your cottage and thus, into your body, they are your guests. They do what you want them to and nothing else."

"Oh." I took a sip of my wine. "So I can have up to five guests come in. One for each day?" The thought was alarming but interesting. Or maybe it was the wine and the weed.

"No. You can have up to five at a time. All day, every day."

I almost choked again, but wound up swallowing hard. "All day?"

She nodded and took a toke. "Whomever you invite in stays until you tell them they can go. So if you invite all five in, you can keep all five for the entire seven days or whatever you choose."

"Wow." I tried to get my mind around it. Maybe I took a wrong turn somewhere. This couldn't be the same spa Cheryl went to. But then I thought about that. Cheryl was, if nothing else, a true flirt. She talked incessantly about her latest dates and conquests. I can remember listening to her during lunch and the occasional dinner, wondering when she found the time to shower.

I took another sip of wine and looked at Tabitha, thinking that I would definitely *not* be inviting five men to my ass.

"So! Having said all that, Davis will be coming in a few minutes to get you fitted."

"Davis?" I sputtered and wiped my bottom lip. "Who's Davis? And fitted for what?"

"He's your tailor." Tabitha stood up. "He'll explain the fitting process. Feel free to call me if you have any other questions, and when you're ready, dial one on your phone to place your order according to the measurements he leaves with you."

She walked to the door and when I opened it, a golf cart pull up beside my car.

"Oh!" Tabitha turned back with a smile. "There he is now!" She leaned over and whispered. "If you want to give him some pussy, feel free. I hear he's quite good."

I think my mouth fell open one more time as she winked at me and walked out. I stood in the doorway and watched a tall man greet her with a smile and a nod as they passed each other.

He wore a black and yellow guayabera, open at the neck, above calf-length cargo shorts and leather sandals. He had a relaxed but authoritative way about himself, as if he were Zeus surveying the Olympian gardens.

Before I could deny needing a tailor, he was standing in front of me. My reaction to him was instant and mindboggling in its sheer intensity.

At the time, I couldn't think why I would be suddenly speechless. I only know that Davis had such a presence about him that immediately I knew he was beyond any man I'd ever met. My heart started pounding. I felt out of place and distracted, and had to restrain myself from reverting back to my childhood habit of biting my lower lip.

Davis exuded power and confidence in his stance alone. It didn't help that he was rakishly handsome. But he wasn't the first handsome man I'd ever met, so that wasn't the issue.

There was something so *alpha* about him that I felt like he rang a bell somewhere inside me. I looked away to get my bearings but the sound of his voice pulled me back.

"Hi." He grinned. "My name is Davis Chutely. But feel free to call me Davis."

I nodded and stepped aside to let him in. His voice was deep, but had a gentle and reassuring timbre.

He had warm brown eyes that led to an open and friendly face. His hair was jet black and cut low but not short. On each side it dusted the top of his ears, and although it was tapered along the back of his neck, there was just enough of it to dance across his forehead.

For a face that appeared congenial, his thick eyebrows gave the impression of mischief. His nose was straight and well behaved, in contrast to the dark but somewhat thin mustache below that appeared to compete with its wayward brothers above.

I looked up at him as he passed me and a barely controllable urge to lick his full and luscious lips almost knocked me over. He gave me a sideways glance, still with an impish smile.

I stood there by the doorway, watching his carefree progress into the cottage, and couldn't figure out what was wrong with me. I had never wanted to kiss a man as badly as I did at that very moment.

And there was the disquieting feeling that he was familiar to me. But why would he be? Surely I would've remembered feeling someone like him in my atmosphere before. And seemingly charming and handsome men like him didn't fall off trees every day.

A large black case dangled from the end of his right hand. He walked over to the couch and laid it on the coffee table. He turned and looked at me with his brows raised just before he sat down.

"Oh." I closed the door and sat opposite him on the chaise.

"I see Tab left a gift for you." He reached into the ashtray and relit the joint.

I nodded, still baffled by the combination of Tabitha's information, one toke too many of some seriously potent ganja, and a couple of hypoxic moments from all the choking.

"She may have forgotten to mention that I wear many hats here at the spa."

I watched him open the case as I nodded like a marionette.

"One of them," he said, "is that I will be the tailor who gets your measurements for successful orgasms. And the other is that when you're here I can be requested as a guest."

I leaned over and looked into the suitcase and almost choked again. Well, maybe I actually did for a second or two.

Davis looked up at me. "Don't worry, I have plenty of lubricant. And as you can see, all of these dildos and plugs are new." He opened a tall bottle of clear fluid. "And the ones that fit and please you best—you get to keep them. You can either leave them here for the next time you visit, or take them home for personal use." He grinned that sly little boy grin again. "I recommend that you use them with your invited guests while you're here and then take them home and ask for a refit next time." He winked.

I looked down into the case. "Oh my God."

"You can take your robe off if you want to."

He opened the packaging around a rather large-looking dildo.

I could feel my heart galloping in my chest and in spite of my earlier thoughts of bravado, I looked at him with that apparatus in his hand and wanted to run right through the door. Doorknob optional.

His hands stopped moving and he frowned. "Are you okay with this?"

Stupefied, I shook my head.

Davis walked over and knelt on the floor in front of me. Even kneeling, he towered over me. Then he sank down onto his heels until we were eye to eye. His eyes were the brown of a lion's mane. They reminded me of the Arizona desert I'd left behind.

"Sydney." He took my hands in his. "Everything that happens here is consensual."

I nodded and wondered if he could hear my thundering heart.

"Anything that you don't want to happen, won't happen."

He rubbed my wrists. His hands were so warm.

"Do you understand?"

"Yes," I whispered.

"Are you scared?"

I shook my head because that wasn't exactly right. I wasn't scared. He practically emanated convivial coziness, so that wasn't it.

"What is it?" He gave me an encouraging look.

He was still rubbing his thumbs across my wrists and it helped. A lot. I looked away from him and wanted to find a way to tell him that I loved sex. I loved the intimacy of it, the excitement of foreplay, the physical exertion of working equally toward a happy ending, the glowing exhaustion and the satisfaction of a nap afterward. But having group sex with a bunch of strangers was some *new* shit! For me, anyway.

"I…"

I'm a geek! I wanted to shout. *A number cruncher! I wear long skirts in the summer and wool slacks in the winter! It took me two days to watch 9 1/2 Weeks because I was so embarrassed! And I was alone! How in the hell am I gonna open my legs and just let you go to town on me without a second thought?*

I tried to say *something.* "I'm…"

All I could do was shake my head. My evaporating nerve clutched the words I wanted to say and held them hostage behind my ribcage, next to my over-stimulated heart.

"Nervous?" he asked.

"Yes!" My admission came out in a great whoosh that ended in a whisper.

If what I was feeling just then could have been summed up in a mere word—if such a feeling could've been measured, whittled down, neatly packaged and expressed in just a slight utterance of the English language—that was as close to the truth as my boggled mind could get. Nervous.

"Do I make you nervous?" Davis asked.

I looked into those warm lion's eyes and couldn't put my finger on *how* he made me feel. "No." I felt…jittery. Like I didn't know what *I* was going to do next.

"Okay." He nodded. "Good."

I relaxed a little more as his warm hands worked a slow mojo on my wrists and palms.

"I want to introduce you to what's possible here."

My frozen digits locked onto his in a white-knuckled death grip.

"You can say no if you want to." He let my hands go and reached behind me to place his fingers against the small of my back.

"If you need time to digest everything and think it over, I'll understand."

His hands began a slow massage through the robe and it felt *wonderful.*

"But I hope you don't. If you agree, I think you'll enjoy it."

The kindly lion's eyes looked into mine. I don't know if it was his hands, his eyes, or, once again, the wine and the weed, but "I agree" fell out of my mouth before I could snatch it back and swallow it whole.

Davis smiled and it looked like the sun had just come out. His eyes crinkled at the corners and his lips parted to reveal perfectly even white teeth. Even his mustache looked happy. He stood with his hands on my back and pulled me up off the chaise gently. I think my feet left the floor for a second, but I didn't wobble. And it was strange the way he practically undressed himself as he held my hand and led me to the bedroom.

By the time we got there, he had tossed his belt to the side, his shirt was unbuttoned and he shrugged it off quickly. Immediately after that, in the flash of an eye, his shorts were down around his ankles. I watched in amazement as he kicked them up into the air and caught them with one hand before tossing them onto the foot of the bed. He turned away from me and lickety-split, dimmed the lights with the switch beside the door. I looked at him when he turned back and all I could think was, *Whoa.*

His broad and muscular chest was covered in a maze of thick—and I was soon to discover, soft—black hair that thinned on its way down to barely cover flat, strong abs and sinewy hips. His legs were long and as strapping as the rest of him. His skin was a beautiful bronzed vanilla that looked like I could dip my fingers into. I let my eyes travel downward and bit my lip with what should've been excitement, but really was my word of the evening—nervous.

Davis was thick and hung like a proud brother. I watched him reach into the nightstand drawer and pull out a condom. He was as stiff as a board by the time he put it on.

Oh my God.

I closed my eyes and turned my face away as he put his hands around my waist. I didn't and probably couldn't have said a word as he loosened the belt and opened my robe. I shivered as he caressed my shoulders and helped it fall to the floor.

I'm not ashamed of my body. My hips are a little wide but not overly so. My legs are longer than they should be for somebody who measures a mere five feet six inches, and my breasts are firm.

I love yoga and the relaxation that it gives, but it's the only class I take at the gym. Every week I plan to try the spin class and kickboxing, but I never have. So my thick thighs and bubbly ass win the fight against every salad I eat. Since college, I've tried not to obsess over the shape of my body. In my humble opinion, feeling good is always more important than striving to look like somebody else. *I'm thick, I'm healthy, and I love the body God gave me* is my daily mantra. But as Davis stared intently at my exposed form, I felt incredibly *naked* and kept my eyes averted.

"I know something you don't," he said.

I looked up to see him grinning. "What's that?"

"You're gonna love everything I do to you."

He was still grinning when he put his hands around my waist and lifted me onto the bed. And you know what? He was as right as rain. He laid me down on my back and stretched himself out above me and leaned his face close to mine.

That man kissed me so well, so slowly and so passionately, that I forgot about who he was, what I was doing there, that his penis looked like the business end of a mini-bat. I forgot all about everything.

Davis kissed me like I was the dessert after a fulfilling meal and he needed my sugar rush before he got up from the table.

My soul pooled around us and evaporated into bliss as he pressed those incredibly soft yet firm and lush lips on mine and thrust his tongue into my mouth.

I sighed as my timidity and my *nervousness* melted away. I wrapped my arms around his neck as he used his hips and his legs to spread my thighs apart. I was so grateful when he used those incredibly big hands to rub and touch my body until I practically *ached* between my legs. Not once during those first few moments did he rush me. Not once did he rush himself, like some men who are impatient and can't wait to unwrap the sweet treat beneath them and then greedily run through it in a hasty effort to get to the center of the roll of the Tootsie Pop.

Not that man. Not once did he try to arrive early. I should've known who I was dealing with, even then.

Davis savored my skin as he licked and then lightly kissed my chin and my throat, before lazily taking one breast between those expert lips.

"Ooohhhhh…" I heard and couldn't believe that it was me who was moaning and arching myself up to meet his mouth. My nipples were so hard they *hurt,* and I damn near *thanked* him when he sucked and licked and gently pulled on the skin on the underside of my breast with his teeth.

I couldn't believe that it was me who was ready first. I wanted him to have every limb, both thighs, both breasts, both butt cheeks and every inch of myself as I pressed my body up against his. He damn near killed me, taking his time.

I was ready when his hand reached between us and covered me completely. I was ready when he pressed and then rubbed his palm over my clitoris. I can't recall ever being so hot and so riled up in the history of my life.

He had me exactly where he wanted me. Had he said "Go rob a bank," I would've looked for a gun. Had he asked me my name, I would've come up blank. But he didn't say a word.

He moved himself up slowly and slid his member between my legs and into my body with such ease and casualty that I didn't have time to think. I didn't have time to remember. I was hot and wet and ready. He must've known, because he slid himself inside me in one clean stroke.

I gasped in a great rush of air and couldn't let it go. I trembled in shock and amazement as he filled every inch of space and time and pushed beyond boundaries that I didn't know I had. He spread, and spread, and *spread me,* further still, as he made himself known to the furthest reaches of my body until I felt *small.*

Davis put his mouth over mine and gently blew in what I needed, and I remembered to exhale. In one fell swoop that man filled me completely and I couldn't think or feel beyond him, nor could I verbalize my astonishment at how thoroughly he *occupied* me and left no room for anything else.

"Ahhhhhh..." He moaned in my ear. "You're as tight as a drum."

I couldn't speak, utter a word, neither accept nor deny him as he put his hands beneath my shoulders and pulled me closer. I wrapped my arms around his neck and pressed my face into his throat.

He moved slowly, pulled his hips back just a little, and I sighed and then gasped in shock as he brought them back once more. And again, and again, until he began to stroke me in an even and measured rhythm.

He took his time as my body stretched and squeezed, widened and contracted with each stroke.

"I wanna teach you..." he whispered. "Everything...everything you need to know..."

He moved slowly and I moaned as a flame inside me flared high and lit my being on fire.

"Show you..."

He pulled his hips away and brought them back with more force than he had before. I could hear myself moaning.

"How to please me..."

His voice was so deep, it rolled into my ears the way his hips and his engorged phallus rolled into my body like a thunderous wave.

"As I'm pleasing you..."

He took his hands away from my shoulders and pulled my arms away from him.

"How to please yourself..."

He held my hands in his own and pulled himself out of me almost completely.

"How to enjoy my perfect sex..."

He came back to me in a deliberately slow and forceful thrust. I cried out as he pushed and swelled inside me.

"All night," he whispered. "All night long."

He pressed his lips against mine. I gasped as he pulled himself out and I held my breath until he arrived with more strength than before.

He moved inside me as he held my hands above my head. He literally covered my body with his and moved with a slow and calculated rhythm that felt like nothing I'd ever experienced. He gave me the most exquisite pleasure I've ever had.

I held onto him as he possessed me for what seemed like hours.

I woke the next morning and pressed my face into the pillow, trying to hide from the cacophony of birds calling to each other from tree to tree, as the sun insisted on adoration. I smiled into the pillow and turned over with it. Slowly, I remembered the night before. How *well* he had me!

After the first half hour or so, Davis got up and left me lying in the middle of the bed, exhausted and half-asleep, not even caring that I didn't have an orgasm. But then he came back with a bottle of wine and two glasses.

We each drank a glass and got started again. Another half hour was all I could take. He stopped after I put my hands on his face and told him that I'd had enough. He smiled at me and nodded.

I don't remember when I fell asleep. I don't remember when Davis left me. I can say that the next morning came in bright and sunny and I couldn't stop smiling.

"Maybe." I shrugged as I slid out of bed and walked to the bathroom. "Who knows? Maybe I'll stay another day." But that morning brought its own set of surprises.

I showered, put my robe on and walked barefoot into the kitchen. I was about to look for a coffee mug when the phone rang nearby. I found a cordless on the counter beside the stove. "Hello?"

"Good morning, Miss Cooper!"

There was no mistaking that voice. "Good morning, Tabitha."

"I trust you slept well?"

I sighed and stretched. "I truly did!" I looked over at the clock on the wall. It was only six a.m. Didn't that chick sleep at all?

"It may be a little early for you, but the kitchen staff has informed me that you haven't filled out a food menu for delivery yet, so I took the liberty of calling to see if you'd like anything for breakfast."

"Yes. How about a pot of the strongest coffee you have and a croissant with some butter and a few jelly spreads?"

"Will that be all?"

I could hear the sugary sweet smile on her face. "Yes. That will be all."

"Okay, then! I'm typing it in now and it should be arriving at your cottage in the next fifteen minutes or so. Please take the time to look over your food menu, make a few selections, and leave it hanging on your doorknob for pick-up. There are menu selections for four meals and three snacks a day, but should you choose not to use the kitchen staff at any particular time, just hang a do not disturb sign on your door."

"Okay."

"Oh, and Miss Cooper, please make time to select the services you might enjoy during your stay. Once you have filled out your Desire Menu, dial the number one on your phone and leave it in the envelope hanging on your doorknob. Your wishes will be fulfilled within the hour."

Desire Menu? "Uh…okay." I looked down at myself and couldn't believe that my coochie was still intact after last night. "I will. Thank you."

"May all your dreams come true!"

I rolled my eyes after I thanked her for that wearisome sentiment and hung up. I walked into the living room and looked at the coffee table in shock. Davis had left me a note. And a few toys.

The note told me that he'd enjoyed himself last night and would love to see me again at any time. All I had to do was dial zero and request him by name.

"I enjoyed you too." I grinned as I put the note back on the coffee table. "Maybe I will."

I looked down at the absurdly wide and long black dildo on the table and covered my mouth with one hand. "Good grief!" There was a card in front of it that had one word on it.

Caution.

Below the word were the measurements. I leaned over to read them and shook my head. I looked at the next one on the table. The word on that card was *favorite.*

I looked down at the caramel-colored penis and whistled. It looked like him. I wondered if it was the same size as he was.

Damn, that's a lot. I can't imagine that I was worked over with something like that!

But I wasn't sore or calling for an ambulance, so maybe Cheryl was right. Maybe I wasn't well acquainted with my coochie. The next dildo was the same color and slightly smaller.

The word on the card read *play*. It was not as wide as the other ones, but it looked intimidating nevertheless. The next few items on the table were listed as butt plugs.

"Aw, hell naw!" I started laughing. "That is just taking a joke too far!" As I was looking at the various lengths of butt plugs that he left beside the dildos, the doorbell rang.

"Ah! That must be my coffee."

A beautiful young black woman in a waitress outfit stood beside a small round table outside my door. I blinked hard.

Her breasts jutted directly out of the bra she was wearing, and as I blinked, I realized that the bra was cup-less. It was just an underwire support that held her boobs up with two straps over each shoulder. Her skirt looked like it was made out of some sort of transparent patent leather. And she didn't have on a stitch underneath it. I could see her stuff!

"Good morning!" She smiled.

"Uh…g-good…good morning,"

"Please allow me." She held her hand out and I stepped out of the doorway with, I'm sure, that stupefied look still on my face.

She pushed the small table into the living room as I shut the door.

"My name is Darling." She picked up the carafe and a cup. "How do you take your coffee?"

"Three sugars and two creams," I answered absently, feeling embarrassed for the both of us.

I watched her in speechless disbelief as she walked over to the coffee table and bent over in the process of setting down the coffee cup and the small plate with the croissant beside it.

Where the hell are the rest of her clothes? And who told her that I wanted to see her whole ass?

Thankfully, she straightened up and turned around to me.

"Is this your first time at the Spa?" Darling asked.

"Yes." I focused on a space above her head.

"Do you like men or women?"

"What?"

"Men or women?" she asked with a smile as she walked toward me.

What the fuck? "Men!"

"Well, I'm bi. And you're very attractive."

Darling took another step closer, and I never considered myself quick before I met her, but my hand shot out and grabbed her wrist before she could put hers in the folds of my robe. "Hey!" I stepped back. "What do you think you're doing?"

"I just wanted to taste you."

She gave me a plaintive look, like I had snatched a precious, much-loved toy out of her grasp.

"Whaaat!?!"

"Even though I'm part of the kitchen staff, I'm available in an hour or so if you want your pussy licked."

"Not on your life!" I'm sure my face pulled into a grimace. It still does every time I think about that incident.

Darling shrugged. "Request me if you change your mind."

She gave me a sweet smile, let herself out and left me standing by the door with, once again, my mouth hanging open.

"Damn!" I looked at the closed door. "What the fuck kind of place is this!?"

Twenty minutes later I was pouring my second cup of coffee and going through my folder. The Desire Menu was a thing to behold.

It was a questionnaire on all things sexual, freaky, and in my opinion, nasty as hell. It asked me if I liked bondage, but all I could think of was leather and chains. I grinned and shook my head. It asked me the same question that Darling asked me—what was my gender preference? Or did I have one? Then it went on to a list of options where I could make my selections by putting a checkmark in the box next to it.

BDSM? I frowned and wondered what the letters meant. I was truly puzzled when I noticed the words, *written contract with safe words required*, in small print beneath it.

Top? Or Bottom preference? There was a small box next to both of those options.

Resistance play?

Role play? There was another special notice underneath that one. It asked to please list types of play preferred, and discuss roles and expectations thoroughly with guests before beginning.

I took another sip of my coffee and realized that I was completely out of my element. I thought about getting my phone so I could look half that shit up!

Toilet? *What the hell is toilet? Am I supposed to have sex with someone while I'm on the toilet?*

"Ugh." I shuddered but read on.

Anal sex? Artificial sex? Artificial sex with cunnilingus? Artificial sex without cunnilingus? Cunnilingus from a man or woman? Erotic asphyxia? Fellatio? Fellatio with multiple guests at one time?

"Okay." I put the card and the pencil down on the coffee table. "That's enough of that." I gathered it all up along with the toys Davis left me and put them inside a drawer in the wall unit.

I spent the day in my cottage, reading and listening to my MP3. I ordered a fruit tray for lunch, a salad for dinner, and polished off a bottle of wine by the end of the night. Each time I ordered, I requested the table be left outside the door. The risk of being fondled by Darling completely skeeved me out. By nightfall I had a long, hot soak in the huge tub, oiled my skin to a high sheen, and slept in the middle of the ginormous bed. It was heaven indeed.

On the third day, I decided that I'd had enough of my self-imposed seclusion and would be leaving that afternoon. After all, I could do the same thing at home. I showered and donned my fluffy robe. With my favorite book in hand, I ordered the same breakfast as the day before. I even waited ten minutes after the doorbell rang before I opened it.

"Hi!" Darling smiled. "I was starting to wonder if you were gonna leave it out here to get cold!"

She had on the same outfit as the day before and *I* wondered how she could walk around like that. But then I remembered. The O stood for orgasm. I stood back and let her push the cart in. "I was hoping you wouldn't be standing out there when I opened the door."

She gave me a funny look as I closed the door behind her. I walked over to the chaise lounge and sat down while she poured my coffee.

"You don't want me to touch your special place, do you?"

"I'm not in the habit of letting anyone, least of all a woman, touch me like that."

Darling stirred in the cream and sugar, took the spoon out of the cup and looked at me carefully.

I shook my head at her, trying to figure out what planet she came from, when she walked over and knelt down in front of me. Instinctively, I squeezed my knees shut.

"We don't have to kiss or become lovers or anything," she said quietly. "I'm here to please you."

"You're a woman, and I have no interest or desire in women."

"You might like it if you try it." she said as she pushed the folds of my robe aside and touched my knees.

"Hey!"

"This doesn't make you gay or bisexual or anything. It just means that you like to feel good."

"Don't do that."

"You don't like being touched?"

I opened my mouth to tell her that it was time for her to leave when she leaned back and looked at me curiously.

"Have you been serviced since you've been here?" she asked.

Where the hell did they find these people?

"Have you been fucked at all since you came here?" Darling leaned back and reached behind her to pass my coffee cup. "Don't you have any toys?"

I hung my head and couldn't help but laugh. It was obvious that she was either a sex fiend or truly about her damn gig, 'cause she just couldn't seem to deliver the coffee and beat it. Or maybe that was her whole point. For all I knew, beating it probably came with the meal. Like a napkin.

I chuckled a little more as I accepted my cup and took a sip. Oh, well. I was leaving in a little while and thought I would never see her or anybody else in that place ever again. And a little conversation never hurt anybody.

"I do have toys," I said. "Davis left them for me."

"Davis?" She frowned as she fixed a cup for herself and settled down on the floor at my feet. "Davis Chutley?"

"Yes."

Darling gave me a strange, sideways glance. "He came to see you?"

"Yes. He said he's my…" I tried to remember the word for him. "My tailor."

"Mr. Chutley is your tailor?" She looked at me in wide-eyed wonder.

"Yes." I nodded slowly. "Why? What's wrong with him?"

"Nothing's wrong with him." Darling grinned. "But I can't believe that he came to see you."

"Well, why wouldn't he?"

"Well, let's see…Mr. Chutley is the one who does all the screenings for members. He's the person who makes the final decision for hiring the guest staff. And oh yeah, he owns the place."

"What?" I almost dropped my cup. "Are you sure?"

"Yup." She smiled. "And you say he came here to fit you?"

I nodded silently.

"There are three tailors on staff." Darling frowned thoughtfully. "I wonder why he came to fit you himself?"

"And he…he…"

"Did he fuck you?" Darling sat up and looked at me. "Was it good? Did he give you some? Well, did he?"

"I'd rather not say." I took a quick sip.

"I know what that means. He did fuck you. Damn!" Darling was smiling at me with pride. "Did he offer to be your guest?"

"Yeah." *The owner?* "I wonder why?"

"Well." Darling stood up and straightened her plasticky little skirt. "Call and request him. Then you can ask him yourself."

I sipped my coffee as Darling let herself out. I thought about Davis the rest of the morning. But I didn't call him. Instead I got dressed and was in the process of putting my toiletries back in my bag when the doorbell rang again. *How in the hell can they call this place a spa with all the damn interruptions?*

"Hi." Davis grinned at me.

"Hi." That feeling of unavoidable animal magnetism came over me again. I tried so hard not to show it. I don't think it worked, though.

"May I come in?"

I nodded like a schoolgirl and stepped back from the doorway. I followed him into the living room and sat on the chaise. He picked up my book on the coffee table and raised his eyebrows.

"I was…uh…reading it." I wanted to smack myself for not remembering to put it back in my luggage.

"You're at The OSpa" He carefully laid my book back down. "Alone in your cottage, and reading tax law."

I didn't even try to defend that. I nodded again and felt like the geek that I really am.

"See anything wrong with that picture?" he asked with a devilish grin.

I bit my lip and shrugged.

"Are you not able to enjoy yourself?"

"I…I did." I thought about the way he made me feel a few days ago. "It's just…I can't go through with all this."

Davis stared at me and I tried to collect myself. I knew I had the ability to think clearly. And I did my best. "How did you know I was alone in here?"

"Darling told me."

"Oh." I rolled my eyes. "She's got a big mouth."

"Yeah. And she prides herself on it."

He smiled at me and I couldn't help but smile back.

"Do you feel like having some company today?" he asked.

I remembered how he felt inside me and forgot all about the fact that I was leaving.

"C'mere." Davis waved me forward to him with one hand.

I walked over and he pulled me down onto his lap. I straddled his thighs and wondered what I was doing. At the time, I didn't really recognize what was happening. I can say now why I felt like that then, and in retrospect, my body must've known what was coming.

But at the time I was trying to maintain myself. Trying to figure out why this man—'cause that's all he is, just a man— why this *man* made me feel like I didn't know myself.

How was it that I felt like I might do any damn thing, just because he knew how to work me over? I tried to find something else to focus on when he put his hands in my hair and tilted my face up to his.

"You've been here three days and you haven't made any requests."

I shook my head and couldn't seem to breathe right.

"I want the rest of your time."

He gave me the most intense look I've ever been on the receiving end of.

"Just me, and no one else. Do you accept?"

My heart was pounding. I thought I was gonna shake myself into a million little pieces and all of me would just crumble to the floor at his feet. 'Cause that's where I was, emotionally. At his feet.

He's just a man. I remember repeating that over and over in my mind. *He's just a man.* But my body wasn't listening. My skin was on fire and melting off my frame. My heart started a weird hippity-hop in my chest as my lungs to forgot how to expand and depress so I could keep sending oxygen to my befuddled brain. My hair tried to stand up and touch the ceiling. And even my tongue—usually so obedient, following thoughts and commands without the slightest hesitation—was glued to the roof of my mouth in indecision. It wanted to come forward to betray me with a word.

What word?

After a few seconds, Davis leaned in closer and my heart hippitied while my chest hopped as his lips touched mine. A caress, almost. That's when my mind shut down, my thoughts took a vacation, and the whole blackboard of common sense was wiped as clean as a whistle. I was completely new all over again.

I couldn't answer him. I was stuck on stupid. *Sprung* for the first time in my life, and my tongue went on holiday right along with my self-preservation. It was only my body that answered. I was *reduced* when he pulled back a little and waited. I trembled with uncontrollable excitement and barely-suppressed desire, seemingly in answer to his proximity alone.

His eyes stripped away any vestiges of my resistance, denial, or even concern for that matter. He held me and I just was. Davis leaned in once more and my chest hitched and I forgot that trick again. The one that brings in air and puts out carbon dioxide.

"Say yes," Davis murmured as his hands in my hair pulled my face closer and he kissed me gently.

Only one word came out of the foggy clouds of my emotions. Only one word flashed bright white on the blackboard of my brain. Just one syllable and one thought pushed forward to stand bright enough almost to be heard in the hushed vacuum of awe, surprise, and—dare I say it—a wild, sexual, turn-on that was so strong, it glowed a bright neon *red*.

"Say…"

Davis ran those deliciously sensual lips along my jawline and pulled my earlobe with his teeth as his tongue set my soul on fire with hot licks.

I shivered and finished it for him. "Yes."

He brought that lava-hot tongue back around to mine and kissed me slowly. He invaded my mouth and took over completely, the way the cool, blue glow of a full moon mesmerizes every being it shines on.

"Again," he whispered as his mouth traveled down my neck.

His tongue flicked against my skin and made it *sing*, as his teeth nipped and seared my soul.

I whispered the word that launched the affair that would end my life as I knew it.

"Yes!"

In the complete story, The O Spa, you'll hear raunchy details of Cheryl's first visit. Meanwhile, seduction, in all its carnal positions, draws Sydney back to Davis time and time again.

Until the Assistant District Attorney threatens to have Sydney arrested for participating in and promoting prostitution. She's offered immunity in the case if she agrees to wear surveillance equipment and testify in court against Davis and his crew.

Will Sydney be able to keep her legs open and her mouth shut? Or will her heart overrule and force her to consider conviction with a hefty prison sentence?

Coming soon is the complete Novella, The O Spa.

For Karen
And
Summer

Rock Star

I love tequila. Dark, silver, gold, with a worm or without. I like it with a lemon or a lime and sometimes a soda chaser, but my favorite way is straight up with no bullshit.

Tequila smooths my rough edges while it loosens my lips *and* my hips. It frees the true me from my world created civilized shell.

So you know I had a more than a few shots while I got dressed for the concert. I played his top hits, downed a few more shots as I opened up all my powder pots, lined up my lipstick tubes and laid down various brushes so I could apply and perfect my pretty girl face. On the way to the stadium, I was feelin' good, even belted out the high notes in the back seat of my girl's ride. Me, Yoggi, Sha, Nikki, and Unika were front and center in the second row and the show was *all that!*

Me and my roadies, along with hundreds of others, sang, held up our lighters, shook our asses, cried, and screamed while my fifth did the walking between us.

So, as I sit here writing down all that came after, I must admit that yes, I was fucked up to the stupid point, but the show wasn't *shit* compared to the after party.

I was giggling a lot. I do remember that. Some kinda way, my fave, my man pots and pans, my *absolute* sex symbol was standing in front of me in some backstage room, and I couldn't stop giggling like a kid.

I kept expecting some steroid dude to rush in and throw me through the door, but not even my girls were anywhere in sight.

I looked down at my ankle boots as his voice poured over my head and landed in the cleavage of my blouse, where it harmonized with my rattling heartbeat.

He said something smart. Something witty. On queue I giggled again. My poor brain was low on oxygen and dried out, so it's no wonder I couldn't figure out how I had wound up with him.

Free backstage passes maybe? I was tore the hell up and still can't really say for sure. Not that I give a damn. He was as handsome up close as he was from a distance.

His smile, his eyes, his *pores* oozed sex.

My rock star. Grinning in front of me.

The room was trying to spin around and take me to the floor. I bit the inside of my mouth and wiped some drool off my lip.

I couldn't stop staring at him.

Me, with a rock star.

The door opened and he walked out into a grey hallway. I stood there, looking stupid I'm sure, while he beckoned me into the hall with him. My feet slid along the drunkard's invisible conveyer belt (Fix your face. You know you've been on it) and he led me down a tunneled hallway, saying he wanted to show me places in the city that most people don't see. Don't appreciate. The grey walls absorbed the sounds of our feet making a run for it.

"We don't need bodyguards today!" He laughed and pulled my hand.

The stadium exit door led to a park filled with benches that formed a circle around a tree. Broken glass was scattered everywhere, and used, dirty condoms laid beneath the edge of a warbled table that looked as if it had been placed there a millennia ago. Small blades of grass peeked through the cracks in the cement.

"There's real beauty here," he said.

The dreamy quality of his presence along with my high did a brusque stage left, like a needle abruptly dragged across a record.

"I don't see any." I said.

The park we were standing in looked and smelled like a homeless paradise. I rubbed the goose bumps on my arms.

"Look." He pointed above us. "Right there."

The leaves of a nearby fully grown maple filtered the new day's light onto the gleaming checkerboard paint on the table. Sugar glistened like tiny diamonds on a discarded candy wrapper. The sun turned my hands light yellow and warmed me when I held them out for a taste.

"Oh." I didn't want to admit that it *was* beautiful. But I enjoyed the unexpected heat on my bare legs when I stepped into an empty ray.

"C'mon."

He took my hand and we ran through the park toward an empty warehouse. We stopped to catch our breath at the foot of a long wooden staircase that led up and up and up like a cartoon. He held out his hand and I was embarrassed but couldn't refuse the 'ladies first' gesture.

I was tired by the time we reached the halfway point, but hurried because he was two steps behind me. I felt his eyes under my short skirt, looking at my bare ass. My feet pounded the wood as I tried to remember what happened to my panties. A quick flash of a load of thongs and bikini's and even *bloomers* littering the stage at his feet earlier, lit up my memory. *Did I throw my thong on the stage?*

I felt him catch up just as his hand reached beneath my skirt and his fingers whispered against the hairs on my pussy. I jumped. And prayed he did it again.

"Hold on a minute," he said.

I faced forward and listened to his zipper creep down, listened to his hands push his pants past his hips, listened as he pushed my skirt up my back before he bent me over. The excitement of gettin' some from *him* made my hair stand up!

"Uuugh!" I had expected him but he was still a surprise.

His dick was as hard as the wooden rail under my hand. He was still while the slick sap of my twat dripped down around him. He hummed and throbbed in my tight place and I couldn't resist. I pushed back and felt him slide forward. It was good, the way his hot flesh stretched and foraged inside me, seeking deeper space the way a hungry animal looks for food. I loved the way his hips pressed against my backside when he shoved his dick in to the hilt. I rocked back and forth on him harder than I had any right to.

It was so good I tried to get his balls in me. I loved the way his phallus rubbed and channeled against my needy walls like sandpaper on silk. It was rough and rude, the way he fucked me like a stranger in an alley, but I smiled when my hair fell in my face as he hammered his way to my g-spot.

We silently rutted while the stairs swayed gently beneath our weight. He was like the sunshine on my hands and legs in the park, he felt natural inside me as I breathed through my nose while he surged toward my belly.

He was good, really good, and when he pulled out I was instantly lonely. The stairs creaked and sighed when he knelt and pressed his nose against the fine hairs at the edge of my coochie.

"Tell me what to do," he said.

I blinked a few times and let that soak in. With a grin I looked back over my shoulder at the park below. The sunshine continued to kiss the tops of the trees though the city was not yet awake. Like a friend who had caught up just to hold my hand, the dream haze of the tequila sailed back in and I was wet and unsatisfied.

"Stick your tongue inside me." I said.

His tongue was soft, delicate. I was throbbing and I needed a little more, I needed something better.

"Lean back," I told him.

I watched him hold onto the rail as I turned around and planted my feet wide on the stairs with my legs spread and my frilly black and white skirt hiked up around my waist.

"C'mere." I waved him toward me, put my hand beneath his chin and guided his face toward my hungry place. "You need me to instruct you, don't you?"

He gave me an eager to please puppy smile and I pulled his mouth closer as I held on. His lips rested against me and I couldn't wait another second.

"Suck me 'til I come."

"Yes please." He nodded.

It was glorious, the feel of his tongue, his fingers inside me, his mouth gobbling, sucking, drinking me in fifty feet off the ground under the bold blue skies.

A rock star licking my pussy.

"I want you to fuck me again when you're done," I breathed as I massaged the back of his neck. "When we get in the building, I want you to fuck me. Hard."

"Yes please."

His nose, his cheeks, his mouth glistened with my juices. I held my labia apart with two fingers and watched his mouth lock over my clit. I threw my head back and groaned as the heat of the new day's sun filled my body. Warmth spilled down between my legs, my toes wriggled, my thighs shuddered. I held myself out to him as my back arched and after a few more glorious minutes of such personalized lovin', I rewarded him with a climax that was so strong, I held my breath until it was over.

He leaned his shiny face back and gave me a look of such pure adoration that I was amazed. He was sweet-bread dough in my hands and God help me, I got a little crazy with the thought of what we could do to each other.

"Let's go." I turned and ran the rest of the way up the steps.

The door was made of some kind of metal but didn't once protest when I pushed it open. Complete silence greeted us. The room we had reached had to have been five or ten yards wide and just as long. The old, uneven, hardwood floor stretched and warbled toward dirty windows on the far end. The sun felt like it was a million miles away and I didn't want to go far from the door.

I turned around to see him walk in behind me and leave the door open. He took his pants off and his dick bounced up and down.

"Is it my turn?" he asked.

Deep down, way, way down, where nothing but raw emotions, primitive instinct and our true selves dwell, is the capacity to be mean. Even the sweetest, most innocent being on God's green earth can be pitiless and harsh under the right circumstances. You know it's true, so don't judge me because the little boy in him, woke up the animal in me.

A drop of glazed pleasure hung from his tip. I licked my lips but shook my head. I tucked my skirt in the waist band and got down on all fours on the gritty floor with my ass out. "Get over here and fuck me." I commanded.

I knelt there with all my shit exposed, wet and waiting, and I realized that his nether regions was my new playground. I wanted, no *needed*, the feel of my tongue gliding down the sliding board of his shaft, I *needed* his swing to pump me higher and higher until he was drained and I was exhausted.

My rock star grabbed my shoulders, pressed his thighs against my hips and shoved his dick in. He felt harder than before and I grunted under the weight of him. The greedy bitch in me leaned forward and slid him out seconds before I slammed back into him to get the party started.

He moved with a swift purpose and I loved it. His dick was so righteous that I whooped, hollered, and even laughed at times while he rode me like a pro. That sweet stick rushed in and out of me with a momentum that was heart-stopping. I had never been fucked so well in all my life.

"Huhwhoo!huhuhuhfaster!Oooh!huhuhuh…" I closed my eyes against the white-hot heat pulsing between my thighs as he pounded the hell out of me. Each stroke was ambrosia and I let him know.

"Ilikeitgofaster!WhooSHIT!Doitharder!" Sweat poured down my face and my body rocked and rolled to his crazy-fast rhythm.

My rock star did what he was told. He pounded in and out my stuff until it throbbed and protested and I was out of breath.

"Please, I wanna cum," he begged.

"You can cum in my mouth," I said. "Go slow…few more minutes…"

"You gonna suck my dick?"

"Keep fucking me." My pussy was sore but I couldn't let him stop. Not yet. "I like this. It feels good."

"You promise you gonna suck me?"

"Beg." I rocked back against him even though it was the last thing he needed, but I felt mean. My coochie felt mean. That whine in his voice made me want to make him do it to me until he cried real tears. "Beg me to suck you."

"Please! I'm gonna cum soon! Please suck my dick!"

A rock star's dick was gliding in and out of me with the pressure of a shook soda bottle and he was begging me for permission to blast off. I couldn't stop smiling even though my vagina was raw and probably swollen. I sighed and pulled away.

"Stand up," The mean in me said harshly.

I knelt in front of him. His dick was hard and shiny, each vein filled to capacity, the head was tight. He put his hand around the shaft and pointed it at my face.

"Don't touch it, put your hands on your hips."

He groaned his frustration. I stared at the robust prize right in front of my mouth. Another drop of anticipation squeezed out of him.

"Please!" he sobbed.

"Unbutton my blouse."

His fingers fumbled at first but quickly freed me. I didn't have on a bra. No surprise there.

"Play with my nipples." I watched his dick bounce up and down to its own tempo as his fingers tweaked and pulled my titties. I stuck my tongue out and licked him nice and slow.

His hips jutted forward.

"Do that again and you'll put your pants on and go home," Meanie me snapped. He was breathing like I had just whupped his ass, but he stopped moving. "Squeeze them."

He gripped my breasts in his hands as I licked his shaft then sucked hard on his helmet.

"Oh God!" he yelled.

His pain made me wetter and I knew right then and there, that I had missed my calling. *This* was some shit I could get used to!

I took his hands off me and knelt a little further down. "Squat," I said.

His shoes made grinding noises over the silt on the floor as his feet moved apart and his hips dipped. His balls were scrunched up at the epicenter of his thighs, trying to hide. I licked the thin line that separated them.

I sucked his left testicle and tasted myself in the wiry hair around it and listened as he groaned again. I ducked my head down and pulled them both into my mouth. I sucked his balls harder, pulled them down and away from his body with my lips. His breath was ragged above me. My hand traced a line between his clenched buttocks. I felt his legs tremble and I couldn't resist it. I stuck my middle finger in his rectum.

"Aah!" he hollered. "Take it out!"

How many times had a woman hollered like that and begged a man to 'take it out'? I betcha it was more times than even God cares to count.

"Is this the first time somebody penetrated your bootie?" Meanie me asked sweetly.

"Huuuh-huuh—yeah!"

His breath was coming and going in short little bursts as I stretched my neck up. I licked around the hole that was trying to squeeze my finger numb. He moaned and his legs trembled even harder. I licked around his puckered anus and he hummed like a baby.

"You like it?" My tongue went around and around again and again.

"Oooh! Y-yeah!"

I pushed my finger past the first knuckle and wiggled it when he whimpered. I leaned back and puckered my mouth around the head of his dick and pulled hard. He groaned as my finger moved up a little more, and the nectar of his pleasure squeezed onto my tongue as his hips pushed down on my hand.

The sounds of his garbled encouragement told me he was a liar. He *loved* it. I dipped my face lower until I was completely beneath him and my second knuckle disappeared inside him. I listened to his harsh breathing as I sucked and licked the tender skin behind his balls. His legs shuddered and trembled, my lips pulled, my tongue slurped. I liked the taste of him, hot and gritty. I liked the way he trembled above me, like a scared virgin on his wedding night. I liked the delicious sounds he made as the webbing between my fingers pushed against his butthole. I leaned back to find his dick as swollen as a fat sausage.

"Grab my tits," I said.

I took him into my mouth as far as I could. I loved the way his extensive organ stretched my jaws wide as he filled my mouth and tickled my tonsils. He was sweeter than any lollipop I'd ever had, his dick was as juicy as it was satisfying. Every taste bud sang as my tongue pulled and caressed his thickness. He groaned loudly and I decided to have mercy on him. My mouth pulled with a strength that rivaled a vacuum cleaner.

He began to squeeze my breasts so hard they hurt. I dug my nails in the flesh of his ass with my free hand and bobbed my head back and forth like a viper. I stuck another finger in his ass and sucked him harder while he screamed, wheezed and howled as my tongue slurped him up.

My jaws pulled as my fingers fucked his butt hole. I knew he *loved* it because his dick had swelled to the size of a water bottle in my mouth. But I didn't let up. Three fingers wiggled deep inside his vault as my mouth pulled with a strength I didn't know I had.

"Aaaah!Aaaah!Huugh!HuuughGod!"

The sounds of his grunts and cries was more satisfying than the jism that leapt out of him. His whole body shimmied and danced while his hands went slack. I snatched my fingers out of his ass and he shrieked one more time. His hips jerked forward and the last few drops spurted out.

I stood up, spat on the ground beside us, dusted my knees and waited for him to get himself together. He put his pants back on and I took his shaking hand in mine. I was so proud of us.

Back in the sunshine, on the wooden staircase I stopped to look at the few cars in the distance and sat down. The wood was surprisingly smooth beneath my ass.

"C'mere." I stopped him before he could take another step. "You gotta lick me again before you go home." I spread my thighs and touched my swollen pussy.

"Yes, please."

He knelt between my legs and obediently suckled me as I watched the world beyond the park hustle to get to work and struggle through another day of demands.

His tongue was divine. I caressed his soft, curly hair and purred my contentment until my body quaked and quivered through another superb orgasm. He looked up for my approval but I stood up and we descended the long stairs in silence.

At the bottom we faced each other beside a warbled bench.

"I gotta get back," he said.

"Yeah. I guess you do."

He leaned forward to give me a gentle kiss and I reached out and grabbed his crotch. I squeezed a little harder than was necessary and I couldn't help the smile that crept out when he jumped. His dick was hard in his pants again when I let him go and we parted ways.

I sang his shit all the way to the other side of the park and thanked God there were still a few phone booths in the city.

His music is gently seesawing through the air as I finish this. It was important for me to get it all on paper so I could read it when I'm too old to travel and I have to masturbate on rainy days as his music pours over my soul and tells well sold stories about his manly prowess.

For now, I hope he remembers me 'cause I just bought tickets to his next show one hundred miles from here.

For L. Harrington

Well Behaved

1

The ride through Walnut Street, typically a shopper's joyous feast, was marred by retrospection. Kai's narrowed eyes dragged themselves away from the lure of fashion designers and the glitzy testaments built in their honor, to carefully consider the man beside her.

Though she preferred to sip her lunch as she wandered alone from one purchase to another, Kai hadn't been able to resist Xavier's subtle offer to treat her to a mid-day shopping spree.

For the first thirty minutes Xavier had stayed a step or two behind her through leather goods, pre-holed denim and other items that caught her eye, while she had the nagging feeling that her beau was watching more than her figure. Determined to ignore her misgivings, Kai led him into a department store built for shop savvy fashionistas such as herself.

A red pump stopped her and she signaled for the young cutie hovering a few feet away. He hurried toward her with an adorable smile and it was second nature to bless him with one of her own. She didn't miss her stoic lover's brows clashing together when she slipped her foot into the red beauty.

Kai dazzled the young man with another high wattage beam while he stammered on about how the stilettos were actually on sale for friends and family and he hoped she would consider him among the former. She nodded to Xavier when the salesman indicated the register. She didn't miss the withering glare he gave the shoe cutie while she put her pumps back on. She almost asked her crabby companion if he was worried about the price, but thought better of it. It was against her shopper's code to pass up an item she would've bought before the sale.

Her lover's dour mood persisted through her selection of a silken, backless dress that provided an adorable dip just above her derrière. The box of upscale panties that she let him peek into didn't spark a smile from him either. By the time she passed Xavier's driver on the way into his car, Kai had decided to treat herself to a hot bath and a glass of wine. Alone.

She sank into the suede and leather back seat and sighed. In the last year, of all the men she'd dated, Xavier Stanhope was the only one she actually liked. He was an intellectual equal and she enjoyed talking with him. It continually amazed her that she could share *almost* anything with Xavier and he was always nonjudgmental. What made matters worse was that whenever he called, she had to take a minute to compose herself so she wouldn't sound as excited as she felt. Xavier was also the only one who had ever beaten her at *Scrabble* and *Words with Lovers*. A healthy wallet was another trait she preferred in the men she spent time with and Xavier was a brotha who truly brought something besides his devotion to the table.

Kai glanced sideways at Xavier's bourbon hued, noble profile and knew that many women would knock her down to get to him. He was handsome in a silently brooding way, and she felt like the luckiest woman in the world when he beamed that wonderful smile in her direction. He had a body a boxer had to work for, and a member that LaTia would have fondly called an *anaconda*. Even though he was slow and gentle with it. Kai pursed her lips at the shame of not putting such a beautiful specimen to its true use.

Despite all his wonderful characteristics, Kai Burke knew better than anybody, that a brotha who scrunched up his face while his girl shopped, was a problem waiting to happen. Educated, rich, single, baby-momma free, black man or not, Xavier's days at her side were numbered. *I just hope he takes it like a man and doesn't start cryin'.*

The car pulled up outside his condominium.

"Are you in a hurry?" Xavier asked.

Kai leaned into the seat and crossed her legs. "I have a few minutes. Why?"

"I have a proposition I'd like you to think about."

"Okay. What is it?"

"Come up. We'll discuss it over a drink."

"You really need my help?"

"Yes. Your help would be much appreciated."

Kai tilted her head and wondered if her *help* was his way of asking for a midday quickie. "Okay. I can spare a few minutes."

She frowned at his wolfish grin and stopped herself from telling him he didn't need to bring her bags in, but shrugged it off. Carrying her bags was par for the course for any man she gave the time of day to. She sauntered in behind him and laid her hand bag down on the table just inside the door.

"Okay." Kai sighed. "What kind of help do you need exactly?"

"You can start by taking your clothes off."

She arched a sculpted brow. "Really."

Something was definitely up with lover boy. Kai eyed the smirk on Xavier's face as he walked toward her and tugged loose his tie before yanked it up over his head. His jacket sailed to the floor.

"I think I've figured it out." He took off his belt. "But you could've saved me some grief and told me yourself."

Arms akimbo, Kai watched him fling his clothes all over the place. Socks, shoes, shirt, every damn thing. In the living room at that. Prior to this sudden change, Xavier had always carefully laid his clothes over the arm of a chair, or worse still, hung them up before they hopped into bed. He usually looked cute and grateful right before she gave him some, not like a lion freed from his cage. She viewed his broad and muscular body as he stretched a condom over an erection that could challenge a wall. *Hmmm...*she licked her lips and mentally stretched the few minutes to a good thirty.

"Tell me honey" She gripped his tool and pulled him closer. "what is it you think you've figured out?" Xavier's dick was warm and throbbing in her hand, it was all she could do to keep eye contact with him.

"Let go for a second."

Just as she relinquished his penis, Xavier dipped down to one knee and stood up with her dangling over his shoulder.

"What do you think you're doing? Put me down!"

"You could've told me you needed more."

"Xavier I did not give you permission to do this!" she yelled. "Stop this right no—OWW!" He smacked her butt just before he reached under her skirt and squeezed her cheek. "Hey!" A shiver ran from the top of her head to her tingling bootie. She jumped when his hand bounced off her ass the second time.

"But it's okay." Xavier pulled off Kai's shoes and popped her butt again before he reached under her skirt and pulled her panties to her knees. "I don't miss much."

"Who the hell do you think you—" A moan slipped from her lips as his finger slid inside her and stroked her until they reached his bedroom.

She bounced onto his mattress with a yelp. His fingers looped within the front of her blouse and her mouth fell open as buttons flew in every direction and his forearm pulled her into a sitting position just long enough for him to unsnap her bra. It all happened so quickly that she didn't have time to react. *What the hell?* Torn between incredulity and outrage, her mouth fell open when he reached for her skirt.

She sat up as her bra fell forward. "What're you doing?"

"We can stop playing." He reached for her panties still wrapped around her knees and yanked them apart.

Xavier's eyes were smoldering in a way Kai had never seen before, yet he had never looked sexier. She could not deny the sudden heat his unexpected actions wrought between her thighs as he grabbed her ankles and pulled her toward him. She barely restrained herself from locking her legs around his waist.

"What the h—" Her next words were smothered with a kiss as he quickly penetrated her.

His bold and swift presence immediately satisfied something inside her that she could not name. Kai closed her eyes, held her breath for whole seconds at a time as his hips moved against hers. She was shocked to hear her own shameless moans as Xavier went through her coochie like Grant took Richmond.

"You don't appear to be happy." he whispered.

Breathless, Kai held onto him as he pervaded every inch of her body. Sure and firm fingertips gripped her hips as his flesh pressed into hers with an impatience she never expected. She was helpless to stop herself from matching his gluttonous cadence as her body sang a sweet melody of satisfaction. She moaned and dug her nails into his biceps as he paved his own road inside her from front to back.

"I can pleasure you in ways you won't be able" He twisted his fingers in her hair and pulled her head back. "to whisper to yourself in the dark." Xavier's tongue stole her breath and Kai wrapped her arms around his neck and arched herself closer. Lush waves of pleasure spread her thighs wide and curled her toes.

With a flip of his arm he turned her over and his rock hard presence slid in and out with a speed that should've created sparks between her legs. Kai clutched the sheets and cried out when Xavier spanked her on the up stroke. His dick swelled within her and pushed aside thoughts of indignation. She reveled in a rush of heated pleasure from such brash debauchery.

Wide and warm, Xavier pushed deeper as he satisfied Kai's inner most fantasy. To be had with a wild and libidinous frenzy of desire.

Electrified waves of pleasure enveloped her from head to toe as Xavier's fiendish desires quickened his pace. With her face pressed into the ticking and her ass in the air, she was helpless to control the sounds of her approval.

With each lush and pervasive stroke, his expansive penetration pushed against her limits to fill her in places she didn't know existed. She gasped over and over again as Xavier pulled her hips higher and delivered a rapid onslaught like a man gone mad.

He was so thoroughly a part of her that he felt like a vacuum each time he pulled out. With each stroke he came back stronger, harder, and wider than he left. With his sheets in her teeth, her bangs dripping into her eyes, Kai endured the most pleasurable tool of her life as it plowed recklessly toward her lungs.

"I've been real patient with you." Xavier pulled out slowly, then rushed back.

"Uummpff…."

"But you are a hopeless flirt."

Kai's eyes popped wide when his thumb pressed against her rectum. Her buttocks clenched and trembled. "Uuummmm…" The tip of his finger slowly opened the door to a wonderfully new erotic sensation. "Oooooh!" She sucked in her breath as a whirlwind of rapture wracked her frame. Wetter than ever, her walls hummed and vibrated as his thumb slid further in. Her muffled sounds of gratitude filled the room.

"Yeah, it's true I'm wrapped around your finger." Xavier pulled out leisurely. "But before this is over, you're gonna be wrapped around mine."

"Oooh!uuh!uuh!uuh!uuh!" Kai closed her eyes and held on while Xavier knelt behind her and went berserk between her thighs as his thumb plunged in and out of her bootie. The dual stimulation sent decadent sparks up her back that threatened to set her hair on fire.

Beyond the fantastic throes of ecstasy was the thought that she had complained to her friend that Xavier was as sweet as a teddy bear but lacked sexual vigor.

Kai gasped, hollered and moaned as Xavier took his time making a liar out of her.

2

K ai cracked her eye lids and to see Xavier grinning at her. She sat up and clutched the sheets to her chest.

"Whoa, where're you going?" He tried to pull her back to him.

"The hell outta here!" she yelled as she scooted toward the edge of the bed.

"Wait a minute. We have dinner reservations."

"Are you serious? Really? After what you just did—"

"That was an hour ago."

"I wouldn't give a shit—"

"C'mon." He grinned. "You got busted for what? The fifth time? What did you think I was gonna do?"

"Not-not—" She watched a grin spread across his face as he pulled her back against the pillows.

"Give you what you've been begging for?" His arm encircled her waist.

"What?" she screeched. "I don't know what kind of women you're used to, but lemme tell you some—"

"I'll tell you what kind of women." Xavier kissed the side of her neck. "Women who recognize that we're seeing each other exclusively and the door for another man to walk through is closed for the moment. But every time I go somewhere with you, any man who lays eyes on you long enough to get your attention thinks I'm your brother and not your boyfriend."

"You're not my boyfriend!"

"Yes I am." He smiled and tilted her head back against his shoulder.

"Since when?" she snapped.

"Since the first time I came inside you." His lips caressed the tender skin beneath her ear. "From that moment I knew that for as long as you would allow me, no one else would know how tight and good you feel." His thumb brushed across her nipple. "Do you disagree?"

She pursed her lips. "I share myself with you on an as needed basis."

"Meaning only when I need some?"

"Meaning only when *I want* some."

"I'm gonna make a confession." He laid her on her back and leaned over her. "You are the most beautiful and sexually enticing woman I've ever met. I don't want to date, sleep with, or even consider anybody else. Do you feel otherwise?"

Kai stared up into his dark eyes. On their first date she had hardly been able to eat as Xavier watched her from across the dinner table, and it took a serious effort to calm herself. His eyes seemed to be undressing her, his hands touching her, and as each second passed she was grateful for the panty shield she wore. By the time he dropped her off she was a moist and shaky wreck. It had taken days of talking to him on the phone to get over the feeling of sexually breathless anticipation. And he had turned out to be harmlessly sweet and endearing. Until now. Her body was sore and throbbing in all the places that mattered from the best lay she'd had since her first.

"I'll let you know, *if* I get over your outrageous behavior."

He sighed. "I don't want the freedom to see other people." He kissed her nose. "Do you?"

"Move outta my way."

"I can be just as stubborn as you are."

She shrugged. "Whatever."

"In the meantime, do you think you can behave yourself?"

"What?!" Kai pushed him back and sat up. "You arrogant asshole!" She scooted to the edge of the bed as his hand reached out for her and missed. She snatched the sheet around her as she stood up and turned back. "You got me mixed up with somebody else!" She snorted and looked at the floor. "Look at my clothes! What the hell is wrong with you? *You* need to behave yourself!" Her mouth fell open when he laughed.

"You know exactly what I'm talking about." Xavier chuckled. "You flirt constantly—"

"I do not!"

"It doesn't matter if he's nineteen or ninety, when you look at a man with those beautiful brown eyes and bat those lashes at him, he's done."

"Oh please. You're being ridiculous."

"No I'm not." He stood up, stretched, walked around his bed. "As a matter of fact, if you bite your bottom lip, he's putty in your hands."

"Xavier." She shook her head on the way to his bathroom. "I would've never thought that you were one of those guys."

"What kind of guy is that?" He leaned against the door jamb and watched her turn on the shower.

"The kind of guy who is so jealous that he starts seeing and imagining things and before you know it he's jumping out of the bushes straight into my baseball bat!"

"I'm not imagining anything." He stepped in the shower behind her and held his hands up when she whirled around to him, eyes narrowed in fury. "That guy looked at you and I *know* he wanted—"

"That is bullshit—"

"Then you smiled at him and he couldn't get back to you with those shoes fast enough. To top that off, he used the excuse of helping you try it on so he could caress your ankle."

She faced the shower spray

"Tell me I imagined it." Xavier turned her to him. He put a finger under her chin. "Did I?"

Kai sighed as the same old argument she'd had with every boyfriend since she was sixteen got started again. "Basically, you got your ass on your back because I smiled at a shoe salesman."

"My ass on my back?" Xavier leaned back into a hearty laugh. "You need an intervention."

"I don't need to do anything but stay black and die! As for an intervention, if you can't roll with the way I rock, you need to get out the way 'cause there's somebody standing behind you!"

His brows rose. "Oh I don't doubt it. And I am most certainly not gettin' out of anybody's way." He put a hand on both her shoulders. "Seriously though. You never flirt?"

She gave him a dead pan look and shrugged. "Sometimes."

"Sometimes my ass. It happens a lot." He smiled. "More than you realize."

"Okay, so what? It's harmless." She turned back and reached for the soap. "Why do you guys always get so upset about it?"

Xavier spun her around again. "So I take it you've had this discussion before?"

"Well, yeah! But like I said, it's harmless. Don't get so bent out of shape over it."

Xavier's brows clashed as he leaned toward her. "I'm here to tell you that it's not harmless and it is some shit to get bent out of shape over."

"Why?" She put her hands on her hips. "I didn't leave my fragrant panties in his pocket! What's it to you?"

"Kai, you are a young, curvaceous, beautiful black woman. You have a way about you that just oozes sex." his hand dropped down to caress her ass. "I haven't figured it out yet, but at first I thought it was the way you walk, like your stuff is so good that it even feels good to you. Then I thought it was your eyes. You have this way of looking at a man that is so trusting, so curious, and just when you have his attention and he can't quite believe that you're looking at him, you drop those lashes and look away with your bottom lip between your teeth. Like you're embarrassed for having naughty thoughts. I swear to God, it's so intense it's primal."

"No—"

"Yes it is. You did it to me! Even after I got your number I couldn't stop thinking about you. Do you know that's the fastest I've ever called a woman for a date?"

She almost told him that he had actually waited longer than any man she had ever given her card to. Six hours was a record as far as she was concerned. She had damn near forgotten about him until Catrina called to say that 'the big wig from the company upstairs' was asking about her.

"Maybe it's a culmination of everything," Xavier continued. "But you are alluring to say the least. No matter how harmless you think it is, every man you flirt with is almost instantly in love and would move a mountain if you asked him to."

"Don't tell me" she rolled her eyes. "You wanna beat him to the punch and give me the world."

"That's exactly right."

"News flash, I've heard it all before."

"Kai—"

"What do you want me to do? Grow a wart on my nose?" She turned back to the warm water. "If you wanna stick around, you have to get over it."

"Actually, I have a better idea." Xavier put his arms around her and leaned his head down to her shoulder. "I'm truly flattered that other men damn near fall into a swoon when you look at them. So I've decided to make the most out your sometimey flirting. It'll be a perfect way to get to know each other better."

Kai turned around with narrowed eyes. "Meaning what?"

"Every time I catch you blatantly flirting with some guy, I'm gonna replace my suspicions with something better."

"Group therapy?"

"No. I'm gonna take you someplace private and stroke the hell outta you."

Kai covered her stiff nipples with her washcloth. "Am I supposed to be turned on by that crass remark?"

"You want me to believe that you're not, but I know better."

"No you—"

"When any man engages you in an arousing way, I want your body to respond because of what comes after, not because of the person you're flirting with."

"I don't get aroused."

"It's arousing for the guy you're flirting with. Listen, I don't wanna argue with you all the time and I damn sure don't want this to be over. I love the way you feel and I enjoy spending time with you. You're intelligent, independent and we keep each other good company. But I don't want you to ignore me or forget that I'm completely smitten with you. And this way, instead of being mildly annoyed, I'll look forward to it. So whether or not you get to keep your new panties intact tonight is entirely up to you."

"Let go." She pushed against his hands.

"So you're gonna deny me the opportunity to anticipate your bad behavior?" Xavier took the soapy cloth from her and pressed it against her midriff.

Kai closed her eyes against the suddenly urgent need between her thighs as his fingers within the slippery washcloth slid down over her pubis. "I'm always well behaved. And I can't see how you would enjoy watching me flirt with another man. It sounds sick and twisted."

"Not if every time I bust you, you're gonna need a new pair of panties."

Even as her body throbbed from the memory of him inside her, she tried to fight the breathless expectancy of his erection pressed against her backside. She couldn't remember moving her hands, but her fingers were gripping his thick, corded thighs. She snatched them away and put her hands under the warm water spray. "You're overreacting."

"We were on our third date the first time I caught you at it and you just sailed along like nothing happened. I thought the stupid schmuck was gonna ask for your number right there at the dinner table. If it wasn't for the look on my face, he probably would have. I was hoping it was just some incidental shit, but it happened repeatedly." His hand beneath the soapy cloth languished its way up the inside of her thigh. "I don't wanna become 'one of those guys' as you said, overreacting to something that may or may not be there. So consider this a game that we're playing. Believe me, it's gonna feel good to you every time." He kissed the side of her neck. "Why I'm suddenly hip deep into you at any given moment is your choice."

"So I should feel flattered because you wanna leave your dick stamp on me every time you feel threatened?"

"If you wanna put it like that..." he grinned. "Yes."

"I own my pussy. Not you."

"It's okay if you're scared."

"Scared of you?"

"Scared that you're gonna get addicted to it."

She turned around and gave him a flat look. "Just for the record, the only thing addictive around here is my twist. As long as you remember that, you'll be okay." She pushed his hand away from her. "You mentioned dinner reservations earlier. I trust you're talking about my favorite steak house?"

"Of course. We're going to have a male waiter tonight. His name is Arnold."

Xavier's wandering hand had found its way between her thighs again and Kai leaned back against him before she snapped her eyes open and pushed his hand off her. "How do you—"

"Every reasonable request is answered with a yes." He kissed her shoulder. "So Arnold is our waiter, and if you can make it through the meal without flirting with him, I won't have to take you into the bathroom and tear apart those pretty lace panties I just bought."

Kai turned around and eyed the smirk on his face. "I betcha they'll still be on my ass when I get home."

Xavier's smile widened when he reached past her for his own washcloth.

3

Kai grinned at the reflection of her new dress and the lavish feel of her new, black lace, panties. She liked the way they fit, cheeky and sexy. She rolled her eyes when Xavier slipped an extra pair in his pocket.

At her favorite steak house just off South Broad Street, Kai turned her head when the maître d greeted them by name and showed them to their table. She perused the menu and decided on a Ribeye with a glass of wine. She looked up to find Xavier watching her with a secret grin that grew wider when he looked beyond her.

"Hello." Their waiter's voice came from just behind her right shoulder. Kai concentrated on her menu as he came around the table to stand between them. "My name is Arnold and I'll be your server tonight. Would either one of you like to begin your evening meal with a drink?"

She watched a caramel hand pour ice water into two crystal goblets.

"Yes." She looked up to see Xavier grinning at her. "Cabernet Sauvignon."

She kept the menu front and center as Xavier ordered a scotch on the rocks before Arnold walked away.

"So far so good," her date quipped.

"Don't do that." She glared at him. "You're starting to look like the one without self-control."

"Maybe I am." He smiled. "Maybe I'm just looking for an excuse to take you into the bathroom—"

"Here you are—" Arnold introduced their drinks and without delay Kai gave her order from the folds of her menu.

She noticed Xavier watching her carefully. With a toss of her shoulder, she ignored his vigilance and turned her charm toward him and she quickly became immersed in a work anecdote he told with his usual fascinating flare. As she tossed back the last sip of her wine, their dinner was served. Continuing the thread of the conversation with work tales of her own, she didn't look up as she ordered another glass of wine and her plate was placed before her. During the meal they discussed local politics and the changes in real estate in the city. She found his take on the new Mayoral candidate refreshing to say the least. Being one of the significant businessmen in the fifth largest city in the country had its merits.

"Remember, all of this is off the record." Xavier said.

"I don't do political pieces." She wiped her mouth with her napkin. "So, even that juicy information wouldn't tempt me."

"Speaking of juicy, isn't your next article all about sexual restraint in relationships?"

She didn't miss the self-serving smirk on his face. "As a matter of fact it is."

"Are you almost done with it or do you think you have to work on it a little more?"

She curled her lips. "Prior to today, you offered me a lot of insight into the matter, so I'm close to turning it in."

Xavier chuckled. "A few things have changed wouldn't you say? Don't you think you should refresh it?"

"Nope." Sugar dripped from her grin. "Miracles typically happen once."

Xavier laughed and a few heads turned in their direction. "Touché! But what would you say if I told you that prior to today, the miracle was me being careful?" He signaled for the check.

"I'd wanna know why before I could appropriately…" Her voice trailed off as she watched their waiter walk up behind Xavier.

Arnold was a young and suave-looking specimen to be sure. Kai lowered her eyes and looked the other way as their waiter turned toward her. Smaller hands reached for their plates. Kai looked up to see a waitress beside Arnold.

"Would you like dessert?" Arnold asked.

She smiled. "No thank you."

"We have a wonderful chocolate mousse that's sure to please."

She almost laughed. "I'm sure it's good." She bit her lip and shook her head. "But I'm fine, thank you."

"Indeed you are," Arnold answered.

They stared at each other a second longer before he turned to Xavier.

"And you, sir? Would you care to order anything else? A coffee or another scotch perhaps?"

"No." Xavier stared across the table. "I'm gonna have dessert. Elsewhere." With a flick of the wrist, his card popped into view.

Kai held her breath for few seconds as they stared at each other across the table. She didn't notice Arnold's return and she looked away while Xavier signed the receipt.

He held his hand out across the table. "Ready?" he asked.

Kai looked up to see Xavier's eyes smoldering above a ferocious grin. Her heart started a tap dance in her chest. *Dammit!*

Xavier stood up, walked behind her and slid her chair back with his hand out.

"Come," he whispered.

She lowered her lashes as a shiver caressed her spine and flushed her cheeks. With a shrug, Kai allowed him to help her out of her chair. Silently, Xavier led her to the back of the restaurant to a door marked FAMILY. He pushed the door open into a large, single-stalled restroom equipped with a baby station in on corner, and pulled her in before he spun around and locked the door behind them.

Kai's legs began to tremble, her nipples stiffened, and her panties felt too tight. She forced a sigh as she turned to look at the white tiled walls and the one bathroom stall to her left.

"C'mere," Xavier said.

Kai threw her head back and eyed the man who just moments ago had been calm and congenial but now looked villainous. *Who are you?* She squeezed her trembling hands into fists. She looked around them in obvious boredom even as her breasts heaved with seductive nervousness.

"Do you trust me? Give me your hand." he said.

This is ridiculous! What the hell am I so nervous about? It's not our first time! After a few seconds Kai placed a shaking hand in his. He pulled her close enough to touch before he let her go. She wanted to say something flip and cavalier in the face of his audacity, but closed her eyes as her body purred in response to his fingers beneath her dress. Her panties tore like wet tissue paper. Kai forced her breath through her nose when she felt his hand between them loosening his pants.

"We still have an agreement?" Xavier asked as he pulled on a condom.

"Do you think your jump shot can handle a standing position?"

"So far we're 1 and 0." he whispered.

With an arm around her waist he pressed her into his solid erection. She rolled her eyes and sighed again when he picked her up off her feet.

"No." Her heart beat a rapid staccato in her chest. "We're more like five to one."

"Then it's time for a game changer."

The tiled wall behind her was cool against her back. She gasped and pressed her face into his shoulder when he swung up inside her.

"I'm glad you couldn't help it." Xavier growled low in his throat as his hips rocked against her feverishly. "I wanted to take you at the table, I could hardly wait!"

Kai gripped Xavier's shoulders as he held her up with an arm beneath each of her knees. It was the first time she had ever been held that way during sex. She couldn't tell if it was just him or because it felt new, but almost instantly she covered her mouth to stifle her exhilaration as his manhood claimed the breath in her lungs.

Xavier's presence inside her was as solid as it was heavy. He groaned from the pleasure of each thrust as she held onto him and tried not to.

She tried not to enjoy the way he completely filled her from end to end, she tried not to become wet and slick with desire as he took her earlobe between his teeth while he delivered an ever-widening pervasion that was so good it was almost unbearable.

Kai covered her mouth and tried to hold back the sounds of pleasure that escaped her too easily as Xavier came and went like lightning inside her.

She gasped again when he pulled away and let her legs go. He whirled her around to face the wall. She pressed her hand against the smooth tile as he leaned on her back and pulled up her dress.

"Ohhh!" She squeezed her eyes shut as he filled her with an impunity that was heart stopping. She pressed the back of her shaking hand against her mouth.

As her heart pounded and her body stretched and throbbed, his hand beneath her dress touched and massaged her. Her legs trembled and spread apart for him. She fell back against him as her body's betrayal coated his fingers, slid down her thighs and gave him license for more. Her body responded to each thunderous impact while his skillful fingers strummed her clitoris relentlessly.

Breathy sounds of her immeasurable pleasure echoed off the walls around them as Xavier groaned in her ear and his fingers pinched and pulled her. With one hand against the wall and the other over her mouth, Kai succumbed to the wildly illicit sensation of being ruthlessly fucked in a public bathroom.

Indulgence forced her to flatten her other hand against the wall and hold her ass out to him as she moaned in ecstasy. The feel of his broad and perfectly stiff tool, roughly agitating her sweet spot, was simply irresistible. Her belly tightened and she gasped and shuddered violently. Xavier caught her as she fell forward.

He pulled her against him as the sounds of their heavy breathing filled the small room. After he fastened his pants, he spun her around and kissed her.

"We'll finish this on the way home."

"Uh-uh." Fighting to catch her breath, Kai stepped back out of his arms and turned away. She shook her head when he dumped his condom in the waste basket. "Ab-absolutely not in your car. No."

"We still have an agreement, don't we?" He buckled his belt. "Are you welching?"

She scowled. "Back seats are tawdry."

"I promise you're gonna love it." He picked up her torn panties and slipped his hand over hers.

Kai followed him through the restaurant in a daze. Her entire body was hot and flushed and she didn't care that her hair lay disheveled against one cheek. She was grateful for the noisy crowd coming up the block and the breeze that blew her bangs back when Cole drove up.

Her mind wandered as she gazed out the car window, but she quickly turned back to look at Xavier when the curtains started moving.

"I feel like a long ride, Cole." Xavier told his driver as he turned toward her and the automatic curtains slid shut. "Forty minutes at least."

"Maybe you didn't hear me." She blinked at his enigmatic grin as the dark partition between them and his driver slid up. "We are not—"

"Yes I did. That glass is sound and bullet proof." He pulled her onto his lap. "He can't hear or see anything."

"That's not the point! I am not—"

Xavier sighed and pressed the button on the partition again. "We're going to Kai's."

"Yes sir."

"You forgot I was there." Xavier said as the partition slid back up. He smoothed her hair away from her cheek.

She rolled her eyes. *Gloater!*

"This is gonna be a lotta fun." He leaned her back as his hand crept up her leg. "And I'm gonna love every second of it."

Naked beneath her silk dress, Kai remembered her spare panties in Xavier's pocket and realized within seconds why he didn't offer them to her. His fingers caressed and dipped between her sticky thighs until, after a few seconds of shock, the thought of denying him flew right out of her head. Never before had she been kissed so ardently, or manipulated so thoroughly.

Kai wrapped her arms around his neck and pressed her body closer as his fingers explored her.

The car came to a slow stop and Kai leaned back and stared at Xavier in stunned disbelief as he lifted her off his thighs. She watched him carefully smooth her dress over her legs before he gave her a chaste kiss.

No one, least of all Xavier, could've told her six months ago that he had an incredible sexual appetite. She almost asked him if he had taken something that morning.

Xavier knocked on the partition as his lips caressed her wrist. Within seconds Cole held the door for them. The walk to her building was another blur. She wondered if she was wandering through some kind of life-like porno movie when she opened her door and Xavier walked in behind her and locked it.

"Show me your bedroom."

She led him down the hall to her room where he wasted no time disrobing and even less time than that to relieve her of her dress and bra. He helped her lay back as he leaned over her and kissed her. Of their own accord, her legs spread and her hips lifted to meet him.

"No matter who he is," Xavier whispered as he slowly slid inside her.

Kai gasped and clutched his back.

"No matter what he looks like,"

She moaned as he occupied every inch of her.

"No matter what he promises you," Xavier's strokes were slow and measured. "I want you to remember this." He draped her thigh over his arm. "Do you feel me?"

"Yes!" Kai arched her back as each delectable thrust came and went. Her nails dug into his flesh as her body betrayed her once more. She closed her eyes.

"When it happens again," Xavier murmured against her mouth.

"Oooh!" She threw her head back when his teeth nipped her shoulder. "I won't! I promise!"

"It's okay if you can't help it baby. I'm gonna catch you every time and have you 'til you beg me to stop."

Kai could not suppress her pleasure as Xavier salaciously overwhelmed her with the willful intent of a man possessed. She could no more hold back her satisfaction than she could stop her thighs from pressing against his as he artfully brought her body to the height of hedonistic decadence.

Throughout half the night, Kai moaned, whimpered, and lost her breath often, as Xavier indulged himself of her with an intemperance that was sensually powerful.

4

Kai opened her eyes to a new day and looked around her bedroom.

"Oh God. I think," she stretched, "I'm ruined."

After some time in the tub she decided that she was too sore to get dressed. She spent the day in bed sipping tea as one sitcom followed another. At six pm her phone rang.

"Hey."

"Hey girlie!" LaTia's voice chirped with its usual cheerfulness. "I'm gettin' a pizza on the way home, you feel like company?"

"Sure."

Kai hung up and slowly got dressed for her neighbor who lived two flights above her. They had met in the laundry room in the basement three years ago and became fast friends. They spent at least two nights a week talking and laughing over take out. She pulled on yoga pants and a tee-shirt. Forty-five minutes later she answered the door and ambled toward the kitchen.

"Hard night?" LaTia grinned. "Your hair usually looks cute but it's all over your head like you just woke up."

"No." Kai poured two glasses of wine, passed one to her friend. "I've been up all day. And yes, I had a hard night."

"Partying?"

"Nope." She sat at the table with the pizza between them. "No parties."

"So what the hell happened to you?" LaTia took out the first slice and passed it. "You got mugged or something? You look wore the hell out."

"Xavier happened to me." Kai accepted the first slice and passed a paper plate to her neighbor. "And I feel wore the hell out."

"Oh shit!" LaTia leaned back in her chair. "Are you talkin' about the quiet guy with the careful attitude?"

"Yes. But I gotta take it all back 'cause there's nothing careful about him."

"Hold the fuck up." LaTia dropped her slice onto her plate. "What're you talking about?"

"Girl, I think my coochie needs an ice pack."

"Whaaat?" LaTia fell over laughing. "Shit! Is there anybody else at home like him?"

"No, crazy!"

Kai laughed before she gave LaTia most of the details of the day before. She shook her head and poured herself a glass of wine when her story was done. LaTia leaned back in her chair and laughed again.

"He fuckin' spanked me!" Kai stared at her friend, doubled over and laughing uncontrollably. "And you think that shit is funny?"

"Yeah!" LaTia howled and almost fell off her chair. "It's about time!"

"What the hell kind of friend are you?" Kai yelled. "You're supposed to be as indignant as I am!"

"Why?" LaTia slowed down to giggles and reached for her glass. "'Cause you finally met your match? I have seen you in action, little girl!"

"It's just flirting! Why the hell does everybody get all twisted up about it?"

"Cause it's more than flirting." LaTia sipped her wine. "I have seen you turn a man to a puddle. Often. As a matter of fact, I love it when we go shopping together 'cause we get a damn discount when there's not even a sale goin' on!"

"Bullshit!" Kai snapped. "Not all the time."

"When there's a man involved we do!" LaTia laughed again but sobered up when she noticed Kai glaring at her. "Okay look, I don't know what you do to those guys, but that shit works. Within seconds they can't stop looking at you and even after you refuse to give up your number, they always give up theirs."

Kai shrugged.

"So was it good?" LaTia asked.

"Yeah." She tore a corner off her slice. "It was the wildest time I've ever had."

"So that's good, right? What's with that look on your face?"

"I don't…" Kai frowned. "I don't know. I mean…he was too damn confident! Like he just knew he had me in the palm of his hands. And I don't like that shit!"

"Sounds like he had you under the spell of his dick!" LaTia laughed.

"So what if he did? He doesn't need to know that!"

Kai could hardly admit to herself that Xavier had opened a door somewhere inside her. She lowered her head as she realized that he had been so sexually unrestrained, and she had gotten so high on it, that she didn't know if she would ever be able to enjoy regular sex again.

"There was something wrong about the whole thing," Kai whispered. "I guess it was…I just—I don't want him to think that he can control me with his crotch."

"Look." LaTia wiped her face with a napkin. "I know it's scary, getting addicted to the way a brotha works you out, but you had to know it was gonna happen sooner or later." she narrowed her eyes. "Or didn't you like it?"

"Yeah." Kai sighed. "It was a thrill a minute." She shivered as she remembered all the things he did to her. "At first it was...a bet sort of. I wanted to prove a point, you know, that I can turn off the charm when I want to because I'm not a slave to it." She bit her lip. "By the time we hit the bathroom I was determined not to give him the satisfaction, but...after a few seconds I didn't give a damn. I just...I couldn't help myself, it felt too good." She reached for her glass. "Maybe that's what it was. It was *too* good."

"Punishment fucks usually are."

Kai's mouth fell open. "A punishment fuck? Are you serious?"

"Yup." LaTia nodded. "That's what that was. You flirted, he didn't like it, and he was honest. He told you he didn't wanna argue about it, so he ripped your panties off and gave you a punishment fuck."

"Oh my God!" Kai covered her mouth with one hand.

"You never had one of those?" LaTia picked up the wine bottle. "As flagrant as you are about your shit?"

"No!"

"Well I'm surprised. That's probably why you can't keep a boyfriend. You've been needin' one for a minute."

"Tia that is some bullshit!"

"No it ain't!" LaTia laughed again. "Girl, me and Douglas used to argue about stupid stuff and before I knew it, he was all over me. Actin' like he was mad, but really he was turned on by the way I cussed his ass out. Before I knew it he'd be going through my shit like he stole it. And anyway," LaTia continued, "didn't you break up with the last guy, what was his name?"

"Raphael."

"Yeah, you broke up with Raphael 'cause you said he was a wimpy, cry baby." She sipped her wine. "I thought he was a little soft too. Before that you said you broke up with Jacob 'cause he couldn't say no to you. For anything. Said he was following you around like a puppy until he turned a little rabid."

"Yup. Which is why I had to move or kill him. That cukaloo kept jumping outta trees and bushes and shit. I had no idea he was crazy."

"Probably just off his meds," LaTia quipped. "Or your pussy drove him to madness."

"Do you have to be so blunt all the time?" Kai rolled her eyes even though painful honesty was one of the traits she liked most about her friend. "My coochie did not make him crazy. He was crazy when I met him. I just didn't know it."

"Either way you look at it," LaTia went on, "you haven't been able to keep a man because they either can't keep up with you, or the two of you are arguing about your behavior."

"The story of my life."

"Well not anymore!" Her friend smiled. "Here's to the brotha who came up with something better than an argument!" LaTia raised her glass high in a silent toast before she emptied it.

"LaTia, that shit is not better."

"Yes it is!" She grinned and refilled her glass.

"Riddle me this smartass. If it's better, why do I feel conflicted? It's horrible! Like my coochie just takes over at the thought of him whipping his dick out!"

"Because it's exciting to get bent over and spanked while he yanks your hair and fucks you 'til you say Uncle. Or Daddy." LaTia grinned "That shit is the fuckin' bomb!"

"Something's wrong with you."

"You just said you couldn't help but like it."

"That's too much control for one man to have!"

"That's odd, comin' from a control freak." LaTia snickered. "So whatchu sayin'? He took over your will with his shaloinkin?"

"No!" she slammed her hand on the table. "I will not be turned out! It's supposed to be the other way around!"

"Why can't you just give in for once?" LaTia asked. "What's so wrong about it?"

"Because! Because he's...he told me he was wrapped around my finger, but he said before it was all over I was gonna be wrapped around his."

"Okay. So, why does that shit freak you out?"

"Because he *listens* when I talk. I can actually have an adult conversation with him. And he plays scrabble. I can't" she sighed. "I can't fall for this guy."

"It's not the end of the world when you fall in love you know."

"LaTia." Kai put her glass down and looked across the table. "He's got that shit that makes you forget."

"Uh-uh girl."

"Yes."

"No fuckin way!"

"I'm tellin' you, the brotha is gifted!"

"Okay. You really might be in some kinda trouble here. How does he feel about you?"

"I guess he likes me. He calls me every day, takes me wherever I wanna go at the drop of a hat, gives up his money and his car like he doesn't care. I guess I'm good with him."

"What about you? Do you like him?" LaTia asked. "I mean like really. Can you see yourself spending some serious time with him?"

"Yeah." Kai sighed. "I can."

"So take control. If a guy flirts with you and you can't help but flirt back, take your man home, slip a condom on that chumpee and wear him out." LaTia curled her lips at the blank look on Kai's face. "What?"

"Uhh..."

"Don't tell me you're one of those chicks who just lays there lookin' all pretty while your dude does all the work?" She waited a few seconds for her friend's answer. "Aww sis, c'mon! You're the one always writin' about how women need to take charge of their sex lives and you don't practice what you preach?"

Kai shook her head. "I've done all that with him before. But now that he's out the fuckin' box with his shit, I don't know. The next time I jump on that jawn he might beast out on me!"

"Oh honey. Are you sayin' he's too much man candy for you?"

"Hell no! He's just the right size." She snickered. "I just don't want it to be all about him. If I get hooked on his stuff it diminishes my power."

"Not necessarily. It just means you like it. Good dick don't make you stupid."

"How the hell am I supposed to know that? This is my first time having some. And just between me and you, he got a sista shook! So, pardon me if I'm not crazy about tying a string around a tiger."

"Oooh girl, you *are* fucked up! Look, you need to flip the script on his ass." LaTia held up one hand as Kai opened her mouth to interrupt. "Maybe not today or tomorrow, or even next week, but try not to be so scary about it. He obviously digs you and would probably be pleasantly surprised if you jumped wild on him first. And stop being so bourgeois all the time. Don't be scared to show him who you really are. A funny, down to earth, smart *and* sexy chic. And after he gets to know the *real* you are underneath all that designer shit, freak that nucca out!"

Kai laughed.

"Seriously!" LaTia continued. "Once you get into the habit of ridin' that brotha 'till his mouth is dry, he'll hope and pray you flirt with somebody else, just so you can spank *his* ass!"

"That sounds so damn kinky."

"It is," LaTia answered. "But kinky makes the world go 'round."

They laughed as LaTia held up her glass. "Here's to being on top."

"To being on top." Kai smiled as their glasses clinked.

5

During the following week Kai refused to shop with Xavier by her side, and she insisted on making their dinner reservations when they went out. Her pride wouldn't let her answer his jokes about the female wait staff. Daytime hours found her talking more than ever with him over the phone, and every night she made excuses not go to his place or invite him to hers.

The whole bathroom thing was hot as hell as far as Kai was concerned, but it still felt a little whorish. So outside of the usual chaste goodnight kiss, she had decided to hold back for a little while.

It was hard not to miss the question she sometimes caught in Xavier's eyes, but Kai wasn't ready to explore the way he had made her feel. Like a bad girl who needed to be chastised in a good way. She convinced herself that being temporarily celibate while she figured him out was okay.

Friday evening, LaTia called her to see how things were going. At first Kai told her that everything was good. But when her friend wanted to know how she had managed to control herself out in the world, Kai admitted that she damn near lived behind a pair of sunglasses.

"What're you gonna do when winter comes?"

"Hibernate!"

They both laughed over that.

"But seriously," LaTia interrupted. "It's been a week, you haven't done more than go out to dinner with him since the big bang and I'm getting the feeling that something's wrong. Like maybe you're about to chuck him. Am I right?"

Kai looked out her window at the mirrored LED lights of the towering Cira Center. Below, flowed the Delaware River. Above it cars drove westward on Walnut street. It was the usual Friday evening, filled with traffic, music, bright lights and the promise of misbehaving amongst good company. Yet she was at home, not watching TV, not reading a book, or even working on the article that was due in a fortnight.

"Well no. I mean…" Kai sucked her teeth. "I don't want him get the impression that whatever he wants to do is okay."

"What about what you could do to him?"

"What about it?"

"What the hell are you waitin' for? An invitation?"

"I don't know."

"You're a punk Kai. You, holding out on the cookies, equals punishment for the brotha showing you a good time."

"That's not it at all. I just…I don't know what I'm gonna do about him."

LaTia sighed. "Why do you have to do anything about him? Go on a few dates, have sex if you feel like it, don't if you don't and try to enjoy his company."

"It's not that easy! He's handsome as hell, has a body and a unit to die for and it's hard to say no to all that when it's staring you in the face!"

"A unit!" LaTia laughed. "That's a good one! I gotta remember that!" She snickered. "But you're still a pussy punk."

"What the hell is that?"

"A woman who don't know the power of a Kegel."

"I know how to do Kegels!"

"Then you better get started tighten' that shit up! I'm telling you, there isn't a man on the planet who don't wanna be squeezed while you got your hand over his mouth."

Kai laughed again. "Why would I have my hand over his mouth?"

"So the neighbors don't hear him screamin' like a girl!"

"Tia that is crazy!"

"What's crazy is you not doing it."

"I don't know, you sure men like that?"

"Yes! I'm telling you, grab that jawn and rodeo ride his ass 'till he passes out!"

"Now that—sounds like fun."

"Mmmhmm. And if you really wanna be a bad girl, tie him to the bed posts first."

"WHAAAT? I can't do that!"

"Oh my God, you are a whole weirdo."

Kai laughed but sighed when she hung up. In spite of her bestie's encouragement, she spent the night journaling with a bottle of wine for company.

July's late morning sun filtered through the blinds in Kai's bedroom as she cried out while her feet fought the sheets. Behind her eyes, her hands were tied to two wall posts in a candle lit dungeon. Xavier stood in front of her, freakishly covered with pelts of hair, his member out in front like an angry exclamation point, his muscular body heaving with agitation. He emitted an angry roar and held her up against the wall with one hairy arm as he humped her with a savage and cartoonish speed. Kai screamed for more as Xavier growled like a wild animal and bit her throat. They switched positions and lay on the carpeted floor of a shoe store, both naked and copulating frantically while she held on to him with both arms and both legs as spectators hooted encouragement and threw shoes at them.

Kai's eyes flew open. As her heart tried to pound its way through her skin, she looked down to find her hand between her thighs.

"Oh shit!" She looked at her sticky fingers. She threw back the covers and hurried into the bathroom. A cold shower offered little relief.

The phone insisted on an answer as she toweled dry.

"Hello?"

"What are you doing today?"

She bit her lip as Xavier's deep, melodic voice flowed into her ear, dripped over her breasts and entwined itself between her legs. The urge to kiss him as she twisted her fingers in his chest hair caused a bone-rattling shiver.

"Well…I was gonna go to the library but—why do you ask?"

"It's Saturday. Come spend the day with me."

"Hmm…okay."

"I'll be there in a half hour."

"No! I'm not dressed yet. Give me an hour."

He chuckled. "Really? I could be there in ten minutes and then we won't have to leave until tomorrow. We could order out."

She bit her lip as her towel fell to the floor. Her friend's advice to *grab that jawn and rodeo ride his ass 'till he passes out* flashed in mind. She shook her head. "Pick me up in an hour." She quickly hit the end button on her phone. "I am not a punk!" she whispered as she walked toward her closet. "I just gotta pick the right moment."

She chose a beige, sleeveless, button up, cotton dress that just barely reached the top of her favorite cowboy boots. She looked out the window at the dark thunderheads in the distance and plucked a thin, short cashmere sweater out of her closet. After a little eyeliner, mascara, and lip gloss, she draped her favorite British crossbody bag over her shoulder until it laid against her opposite hip. The doorbell rang just as she spritzed her signature scent between her breasts and on her wrists.

"Perfect." She smiled as she opened the door.

Her date smiled back.

"Did I ever tell you that I love your hair?" Xavier reached a hand out to touch it. Her deep brown cropped 'do just barely dusted her jawline on either side. Her bangs dusted her eyelids and gave her finely boned face a girlish flair.

"No." Kai picked up her keys off the hook beside the door. "Funny you should mention it, 'cause I just had it cut the day before I met you. And I don't think I'm ever gonna wear it long again."

"Is it easier this way?" Xavier took her hand after she locked her door and he led her downstairs.

"Much!"

They enjoyed a late lunch at Friday Saturday Sunday, on 21st street. Kai knew all the wait staff by name and was happy when her usual waiter greeted them with two menus.

A wonderful meal and two cranberry spritzers later, they stood on the sidewalk and Xavier told her that he felt like walking. Kai nodded even as she glanced up at the low and heavy, gunmetal clouds. She looked over at his car as Cole pulled away from the curb.

"He knows where we're going." Xavier leaned down and kissed her cheek.

His lips felt so good on her skin. Kai stood on her toes and pressed against him to return the favor. The fine stubble on his cheek was rough and delicious against her lips. She shivered with delight before she leaned back. "Where are we going?"

"A few blocks down."

She smiled and took his hand in hers, intent on a lover's stroll toward whatever 'a few blocks down' held. But Xavier didn't move and she turned back to look up at him. For a split second she felt completely naked as he stared at her like a hungry wolf. Her heart stuttered and she lowered her eyes as she bit her lip and looked away. It was all she could do not to ask him to share a cup of tea in her bed while the rain drummed against the windows.

"C'mon." Xavier tugged at her hand and they walked a few blocks up and headed east on Walnut street. Every time she stopped to gaze through a shop window at shoes, a blouse, or a designer handbag, Xavier held his hand toward the doors with a rakish grin. From 18th to 15th streets, she shook her head.

As they approached Broad Street, Kai noticed the blue awnings half a block away and spotted Cole as he pulled Xavier's car smoothly into a parking spot to their left. Kai looked over at his car and then back at the store. *Shit!*

"Is this where you wanted to go?" she asked.

"Yup. My mother's birthday is coming up. I decided on jewelry."

She had never actually been inside her most coveted store, but knew from the countless times she had stopped outside, that a glittery heaven awaited her beyond the door. They were greeted by a doorman and welcomed warmly. Kai was immediately impressed with the attentive service. She stood beside Xavier as he looked at earrings, rings and bracelets, diamonds, emeralds, rubies and sapphires, until her curiosity got the better of her and she wandered over to the opposite side of the glass counter to look at the freshwater pearls.

"Hello. And welcome."

She looked up to find a darkly suited gentleman standing in front of her on the opposite side of the counter.

"Hi."

"Would you like to try them on?" the salesman asked. "See how they feel?"

Kai looked up at him and lowered her eyes again as she nodded.

"Yes. The bracelet please."

"As you wish," he murmured and opened the case with a key.

"Oh, it's beautiful!" She smiled when the salesman brought the bracelet out for her inspection. She bit her lip and offered her arm with glee and trepidation. The salesman's fingertips grazed her inner wrist and Kai jumped and snatched her arm back. She giggled at the unexpected shock and shook her head when he started to apologize.

"I'm sorry, miss." The salesman reached out again as he held the bracelet toward her. "I didn't mean to startle you."

"It's okay." She glanced up and locked eyes with Xavier. His dark eyes bore into hers with voracious intent. Her heart started a thunderous drumroll and she took a step back.

"Miss?" The salesman called out to her from a deep chasm. "Miss, are you all right?"

The entire world shrunk to a population of two as Xavier held her wide eyed stare. Images of him holding her up against a bathroom wall flitted through her mind and galvanized the center of her body while the moisture between her legs glued her panties to her.

Before she knew she was going to, she was out on the sidewalk, running in the rain.

Her boots tried to carry her away from images of Xavier, his muscular bare chest leaning over her as he smiled, Xavier behind her in the shower, whispering in her ear as he pressed soapy fingers between her legs, Xavier, his eyes full of desire as he held his hand out to her in a restroom just before he tore her panties to shreds.

Kai bumped into a yellow raincoated woman and almost tripped over her dog. She fought to keep her balance as she saw LaTia mouth the words 'to being on top' and the sight of her sticky fingers just that morning, flashed behind her eyes.

She skidded to a halt, half a foot before the corner. She spun around to face the way she came and closed her eyes as the summer rain drummed on her head, saturated her clothes and fell inside her boots.

The yellow raincoat brushed by a little too quickly with the schnauzer tucked safely inside and forced Kai back two steps as the downpour blinded her. She pinwheeled her arms while her heels hung off the curb.

Xavier wrapped his arm around her waist and pulled her back. Angry horns blared behind them and the crowd at the curb jumped out of the way of a knee high splash.

"I—" She leaned into him in the warm deluge. "I didn't—" Xavier pulled her off her feet and kissed her. "Yes you did."

He whisked her off the sidewalk and before she could blink she was in the back seat of his car. He barked at Cole. "Take us home!" The partition slid up and he straddled her over his legs.

Kai returned a kiss so passionate that she wanted to rip his shirt off. She reached between them and rubbed her hand over his crotch. A satisfying thrill shot up her back when he groaned against her mouth. Through the thin fabric of his pants she gripped his dick in her hand and squeezed as her tongue licked his upper lip.

"Yes!" She threw her head back as Xavier's fingers pushed her panties aside and wiggled inside her. Needy fingers looped into the side of the lacy fabric of her panties as she fumbled with his belt buckle.

They hit a bump, she bounced on his thighs and realized what they were doing.

"Wait!" She pushed against his hand beneath her dress. "I—"

"I know." He pressed his mouth against her throat. "It just happened."

"No! Not here." She pushed her forearms against his shoulders as he held her with an arm against her back. "I—I have a confession to make." She trembled and fought the urge to rip her own panties off. "But not here."

Xavier pressed his mouth tight and released her. She could feel the tension coming off him in heavy waves. Even as her hands clutched the fabric of his slacks, she wanted to rub her palms against the wonderful feel of the muscular thighs beneath hers and let him have his way.

She lowered her head and sighed at the realization that she loved the way he felt inside her. Like a wild and beautiful storm that was as frightening as it was intense. She couldn't deny that no man had ever made her feel as sexually liberated as he did.

She tried to fight the demanding need Xavier awakened in her body, even as her body trembled at the memory of his fingers and the delicious feel of his bold erection.

The car rolled to a stop. She could feel Xavier thrumming beneath her legs like earth quake foreshocks.

The car door opened, Xavier got out and held her hand. He held the building door open, she couldn't look at him as she walked in.

"Grab that jawn and rodeo ride his ass 'till he passes out!" LaTia repeated in her mind.

Kai left her handbag and sweater in the living room as she walked through it and kicked off her boots and wet socks in the doorway of his bedroom. Her heart pounded with expectation as she unbuttoned the top half of her dress.

She jumped when she felt him behind her. Xavier's hands slowly worked their way up her thighs as they pushed her dress up to her waist until his fingers looped inside her panties.

"Why did you make me wait?"

"I…"

Her heart started a healthy gallop as his grip slowly tightened against the lace around her. A wild erotic shiver threatened to stand her wet hair on end. She shook her head against his chest.

"Did you think I couldn't be easy with you?"

His body was as taught as piano wire behind her and she could feel the fabric of her panties slowly stretching beyond their capacity. She put her hands over his and squeezed her eyes shut as euphoria coursed through her veins.

"Answer me."

"Y-yes." She hated the shaky sound of her own voice and the way her breath came and went too loudly and too quickly.

"You're right." Xavier rubbed the back of his hands against her hips. "It's harder than I realized. Now that I've let the fiend out of his cage, I'm fighting like hell to put him back."

Kai looked down at his hands and remembered her dream. How he had bitten her. How she liked it.

"Do you trust me?" she whispered and felt him nod against her neck. "Take my panties off."

She licked her lips as the lace in his hands gave way. Sounds of her breathless expectancy bounced off the walls.

"Consider this a game we're playing." She started unbuttoning her dress. "I promise you're gonna love it." She turned to face the hunger in Xavier's eyes.

"Okay." he said.

"I want you to do exactly as I say." A small smile played around her lips. "Can you do that for me?"

He nodded.

"Say yes." she said.

His eyes narrowed. "Yes."

"Don't move until I tell you to." She watched his frown deepen. "Do we have an agreement?"

"Yes."

Kai locked eyes with Xavier as she unfastened the last button on her dress and let it slip from her shoulders. She held his gaze as she unclasped her bra and tossed it behind her. She ran her tongue over her lips.

"I remember when you carried me in here and fucked me so hard that I came all over you." She smiled when his eyes widened. "I tried to be offended but" she unbuckled his belt and unclasped his pants. "to tell you the truth—" She saw his hands move out of the corner of her eye. "Don't move."

His hand fell away as the purr of his zipper resonated around them. She pushed his slacks down and knelt to follow them. With her fingers around the top of his underwear, she stuck her tongue in the slit of his boxers and licked the tip of his dick.

"Uuuh…" Xavier groaned.

Kai yanked his boxers down to his ankles and leaned back when his penis popped out.

"You felt so good inside me." she whispered. "I loved every second of it." She knelt a little further and licked his balls. Xavier groaned louder. "You were as hard then as you are now." She reached down and unlaced one of his shoes as her mouth darted forward and sucked his hood before she let go with a decided 'pop'. Xavier released a ragged sigh.

"Your dick was like a hot battering ram." She unlaced his other shoe and stood up. "Step out of them." She watched an excited grin alight on his face as he kicked his shoes and pants aside. "Take your shirt off." She took a step back and held her breasts in her hands. He grinned even harder when she pinched her nipples between her fingers.

She waited until he stood before her, naked, hands on his hips, while his one-eyed hammer stood out as straight as an arrow.

"Oh!" She smiled. "I forgot something." She turned around and bent over toward her dress on the floor. She looked at him through her splayed legs as his hands reached for her hips.

"Hold it! You promised."

"Kai!" Xavier yelled.

With both hands around her ankles and her coochie spread wide enough for him to see up to her throat, she smiled. "You said you wouldn't move. You're not welching are you?"

"No."

His tight lipped answer gave her all the encouragement she needed. Kai reached into her dress pocket and took out a condom. Xavier began to breathe raggedly above her. She decided to help him out.

"It was so gooood!" she exclaimed as she reached between her thighs and stroked herself. "I was so wet" she rubbed two fingers between her lips and checked to see that he was watching. "and dripping" she stuck one finger inside herself and pulled it out slowly "like now." She moaned seductively as she leisurely played with herself. "Do you want some of this, baby?" she spread all four fingers over her vagina and pulled them forward.

"Jesus!" Xavier hissed. "You are killin' me!"

"You fucked me repeatedly that day." Kai straightened up, turned around and dropped to her knees in front of him again. She licked his balls as his breath hissed through his teeth. "You shoved your dick in me up against a bathroom wall" she licked the fold between his left leg and his groin. "with my clit between your fingers." she switched sides and licked the crease in his groin on the right.

She almost yelled in triumph when he shuddered violently. "You rocked that hot pipe inside me" she grabbed his buttock with one hand. "until juices ran down my legs." She darted her head forward and took him in her mouth and pulled hard with her cheek muscles until he gasped. She licked his tip slowly, before she let go.

"And in my own bed" she let her finger travel down the crack of his ass "you held my legs in the air and made me call out your name" Her opposite hand rolled the condom over his ever widening phallus. "while you ate my pussy like you were starving. You made me come in your mouth." She licked his balls slowly. "Then you put ice cubes inside me and sucked my titties while they melted." She licked the thick vein on the underside of his dick. Her finger nail stroked his anus and he shuddered.

"You were right." She nipped his helmet with her teeth and was tempted to do it again when he yelped. "You spent half the night doing things to me that I can't repeat." She stood up with a firm grip on his willie and licked one of his nipples. The sound of his groan was almost enough.

"I was so sore I had to soak in the tub the next day. It was the best night of my life." She smiled. "Now it's your turn." Still holding her precious cargo, she turned and pulled Xavier behind her until she reached his bed. "I'm gonna be nice though. I'll let you lay down yourself."

She yanked on his dick when he laid on the mattress.

"Uuggh!" he yelled.

"Don't be a baby. You *want* me to pull on your dick." She quickly climbed on top and put her hand over his mouth. "Remember our agreement." She smiled when he looked alarmed. "No touching until I tell you to. Put your hands in the sheets!" Before he could comply or protest, Kai squatted above him and pushed down.

"Aaaahhh…." Xavier groaned.

After hours on end of practicing Kegels, Kai bore down on the juicy candy stick inside her. She shuddered with relief as her muscles constricted on the way up.

"Aaarrrgghhh!"

"Just lately" she grunted as her hips pushed down with incredible force. "You haven't looked happy." She put one hand over Xavier's mouth and gripped his shoulder with the other as she squeezed and rode him with a reckless triumph she never thought possible. "So I'm gonna help you with that!"

She squeezed with savage satisfaction every time Xavier howled beneath her hand as she used her muscles with vicious acuity. Kai yearned for the feel of his fingers and spun around to squat over him with her legs spread outside his hips. She grabbed his hand as she guided him inside her. "Touch me!" she panted.

His fingers obeyed as she rocked and pushed, he pinched and groaned, she strained and grunted. The bed shook on its foundation as Kai pounded herself onto him.

"Press the button baby! Press the button!" As Xavier's fingers did her bidding and he rocked against her g-spot. "Harder!" Rivulets of pleasure ran down her thighs, coated his testicles and helped him slide deeper. "YES!" she screamed when he grabbed her hip. Her bangs stuck to her forehead, her buttocks quivered amid the resonating sound of skin slapping against skin, the moist sucking noise between her legs, and Xavier's deep growls behind her.

"YEEESSSS!" Kai reached behind her and grabbed his hips when he sat up. She dug her nails into his skin as she thrust down on him hard enough to make him rock back for a second. Xavier's fingertips pinched her clit with savage intent as he hammered her relentlessly from behind.

"Yesyesyesyes" Kai pushed down and squeezed. "I'mgonnacomeohGod!"

She sagged against him. They fell back onto the mattress and faced each other. She bit her lip as he stared at her.

"That was amazing." he whispered. "Who are you?"

Kai laughed. "I wanted to ask you the same thing!"

Xavier grinned and kissed her hand. "The man who is hooked on you."

"Xavier...I'm" Her fingers caressed his wiry chest hair and she sighed. "I'm not promiscuous. And I-I don't want to be with anyone but you—"

He tried to stop her with a kiss.

"I don't want you to get upset when—"

He kissed her lips, her eyes, her chin. "I'm not upset. Every man who looks at you sees what I see. How beautiful and sexy you are."

"I-I like the way we are with each other. How we laugh and talk about almost anything, how well we get along with each other. And the sex is insanely good!" Kai grinned and leaned back when he reached for her. She lowered her eyes and bit her lip. "I don't know what's wrong with me, but—"

He flipped her onto her back. "It's my turn to confess. In the beginning I was careful with you." He gently kissed her. "You were all I thought about and I couldn't wait to have you. But I held back because I couldn't quite believe that the woman of my dreams was beside me." He kissed the side of her mouth, her nose. "But then I thought that you were flirting right in front of me because I wasn't enough. So I pretended to be jealous so I could lose it in the best way possible.

"That was the most exciting day of my life!" He kissed her nose and chuckled. "And it was such a relief to have you the way that I wanted to, that I couldn't restrain myself in the restaurant or in the car afterward, and especially not in your bed. I thought we had turned a corner together."

Kai's mouth fell open in shock. "We did!" She whispered. "I loved it! I felt like a complete freak, but oh my God that was incredible!"

"Yeah, but the next time I saw you I thought I had gone too far, that maybe I'd scared you off." Xavier smiled against her mouth as he kissed her again. "I wanted the chance to show you that I could be good, that I could be gentle. But you ran away from me at the end of every night. I wound up regretting every minute of it because I couldn't touch you.

"I'm so glad that you could be honest and tell me how it feels. Because it's so easy for me to lose my inhibitions with you. I'm still trying hard not to become some kind of wild barbarian who can't control himself."

Kai gasped and held her breath as he slid inside her.

"But the truth is…" Xavier groaned as she pulled him into her. "I am and I can't. Not with you."

Kai arched her back and gripped the sheets as Xavier silenced all thoughts of anything and everything but him. As the images of her dream and the way she awakened flashed behind her closed eyes, she wrapped her legs over his as their bodies smoothly blended.

Xavier held her close as he moved slow and deep. He engaged her body in a rhythm that was as momentous as it was affectionate.

Once again she was shocked as he took his time and moved inside her at a patient pace, yet she felt no less consumed. With each powerful stroke he pulled her closer.

He was no less overwhelming as he took her breath away with each evenly measured thrust. She pressed her face into his neck and even as her body stretched to accommodate him, she yearned for more.

"I'm so in love with you," Xavier whispered. He groaned as her hips lifted to meet his, and her tongue licked and teased his lips as she squeezed him. "Ahh shit!"

Within seconds they lay facing each other with her leg draped over his hip. Their tongues explored and played with one another, their hands clutched and pulled, their bodies clashed amid wet and provocative sounds.

Xavier pressed his fingers into the soft flesh on her bottom as her teeth nipped his throat and her fingers pulled his chest hair and tweaked his nipples. She immersed him in unbelievable passion as he pushed deeper inside her and consumed her with the insatiability of a warrior.

"Again! Say it again!" She touched his face as he leaned in and kissed her with those wonderful words on his lips.

"I love you," Xavier whispered. "I love you."

Kai vibrated with an unspeakable joy each time she heard it. She smiled against his mouth and held on with both arms and both legs as he whispered it over and over again.

The following afternoon, Xavier took Kai back to the jewelry store on Broad Street. He held her hand as they passed the silver and gold display case to the other side of the glass-enclosed counter. The same gentleman awaited them.

"Are you ready to try it on?" the salesman asked.

Xavier watched a slow smile spread across Kai's face. When she bit her lip and hesitated for just a few seconds before she held her arm out, he realized something. Kai's sudden look of joy barely held in check was all about the pearls and nothing else.

"Yes!" She beamed. "I'm ready!"

Xavier almost laughed at the rapture on her face when the bracelet was finally clasped around her wrist.

"It's beautiful," she whispered.

"Not as beautiful as you." Xavier said.

He didn't care one whit that the salesman nodded his agreement.

Kai spent the evening straddled over her beau, wearing nothing but her new pearl earrings and her pearl bracelet as her breasts bounced jubilantly on either side of a twenty-four-inch pearl necklace.

Leave your comments, thoughts, reviews
and perhaps a confession of your own at
#NotYourDaughter'sRomance or on the website
www.eroticaforever.com where imagination sparks action.

www.ingramcontent.com/pod-product-compliance
Lightning Source LLC
Chambersburg PA
CBHW030226180626
46810CB00008B/2994